'Was it that you fell for someone? Or maybe you just decided that motherhood was what you wanted after all? Did something go wrong?'

Allison gave a faint, ironic smile. 'You could say that. Although, as it turns out, I've discovered that Connor is the most precious thing in my life, so I really don't have any regrets on that score.'

He was silent for a moment, but then he placed his hands on her upper arms, drawing her towards him. His hold on her was gentle, but firm, as though he would keep her near to him.

'Does it matter?' she said. 'It was all a long time ago, and I made a mistake. I wasn't going to see Connor's father again, and I didn't want to compound that mistake by involving anyone else in my problems.'

He frowned, looking into her eyes, and just then the door opened. Taylor let go of Allison. She was very still for a moment or two, trying to absorb the fact that he was no longer holding her close, and doing her best to calm the hammering of her heart. She didn't know why he had this effect on her, but whenever he was near he made her want what she couldn't have.

When **Joanna Neil** discovered Mills & Boon®, her life-long addiction to reading crystallised into an exciting new career writing Medical™ Romance. Her characters are probably the outcome of her varied lifestyle, which includes working as a clerk, typist, nurse and infant teacher. She enjoys dressmaking and cooking at her Leicestershire home. Her family includes a husband, son and daughter, an exuberant yellow Labrador and two slightly crazed cockatiels. She currently works with a team of tutors at her local education centre to provide creative writing workshops for people interested in exploring their own writing ambitions.

Recent titles by the same author:

EMERGENCY AT RIVERSIDE HOSPITAL
THE LONDON CONSULTANT'S RESCUE
THE EMERGENCY DOCTOR'S PROPOSAL
HER BOSS AND PROTECTOR
THE LONDON DOCTOR

THE CONSULTANT'S SURPRISE CHILD

BY
JOANNA NEIL

MILLS & BOON®
Pure reading pleasure

First published in Great Britain 2007
Large Print edition 2008
Harlequin Mills & Boon Limited,
Eton House, 18-24 Paradise Road,
Richmond, Surrey TW9 1SR

ISBN: 978 0 263 19940 6

Set in Times Roman 16¼ on 20 pt.
17-0308-54741

Printed and bound in Great Britain
by Antony Rowe Ltd, Chippenham, Wiltshire

THE
CONSULTANT'S
SURPRISE CHILD

CHAPTER ONE

'ARE you sure that you don't mind doing this for me, Rhea?' Allison was busy gathering together her medical pack as she spoke, but her green eyes were troubled as she looked at her friend. 'I hate to impose on you like this at such short notice.'

'That's OK. Don't worry about it. Even though it's your day off, you can hardly ignore a callout to a major accident, can you? I just hope that you'll be able to help those poor people in some way. I told you I'd help out at any time.' Rhea shook her head, making her chestnut curls dance. 'Anyway, it's no problem. I was planning on taking Poppy out for a visit to Rembrandt Gardens at Little Venice this afternoon—it's a beautiful spring day, and I'm sure Connor would love to come along there with us.' She looked fondly at the children, whose ears had pricked up at the sound of their names. 'We could take a picnic with us,' she suggested. 'Would you like that?'

Five-year-old Poppy clapped her hands together, performing an excited little jig. 'A picnic? Oh, yes…yes. I'd love it.'

Connor was a touch more reserved in his judgement. He stopped playing with his toy soldiers and began to roll them lightly between his fingers as he mulled over the prospect. 'Would we have ice cream and pop?' he wanted to know. 'And biscuits? Those little ones with jam and smiley faces—I like those.' He looked at Rhea with wide grey eyes, his mouth puckered in expectation. Clearly, her answer was going to make all the difference.

Rhea nodded. 'Oh, yes, I expect we can manage that,' she murmured, and was rewarded with a cheerful grin.

She glanced at Allison, saying with a smile, 'We'll probably take a walk along the canal towpath later on and look at the boats.'

'Thanks, Rhea.' Allison relaxed a little and paused, looking around to see if anything else needed to go in her bag. 'I'll feel better, knowing that Connor is safe with you. I'm not sure how long I'll be out, but it may be a few hours.'

'That's all right.' Rhea's expression sobered. 'It must be awful, what's happened in the City. You just never imagine these things can come about, do you? Didn't you say it was an event at a gallery—a special exhibition of artwork?'

'That's right. Apparently the ceiling and part of the mezzanine floor came down. They don't know how many people have been injured.'

Rhea grimaced. 'Do you think Taylor will be there—attending the accident, I mean? I should imagine they would have called in as many doctors as are available.'

Allison frowned. 'I don't know.' It was something that had been worrying her. 'I'm not even sure whether or not he's arrived in London yet, or if the changeover will come about at all. This new post of consultant only came up unexpectedly when my boss decided at the last minute to take up the offer of a sabbatical in the States. I know Administration wanted Taylor but, from what I heard, he was undecided about the job.

Anyway, whatever the outcome, he wasn't expected to start work for another week. I suppose there must be a lot of loose ends to be tied up at his old hospital.' She pushed a wayward strand of her long fair hair behind her ear. 'I still can't get used to the idea that he might actually turn up.'

Rhea made a sympathetic sound. 'It will be difficult for you, won't it, seeing him again after all this time? I don't suppose he has any idea that you're working at King's Bridge Hospital?'

Allison shook her head. 'There's no way he would know that. I haven't seen him or heard from him in five years.'

Rhea's gaze shifted, to follow four-year-old Connor, who at that moment took it into his head to chase after Poppy, heading out through the kitchen door and into the garden.

'Give me my soldier back,' he shouted.

'Shan't.'

Allison went into the garden to investigate. The little girl was waving the toy aloft, baiting Connor.

'You poked me with it and I'm going to throw it away.'

Connor glared at her. 'Didn't. It was a accident. You pushed me.'

'Here we go,' Rhea said with a wry smile, coming to join Allison. 'It looks as though the fun and games have started already. I'd better go and sort things out.'

Allison's brow furrowed. She walked over to her son and said in a quiet voice, 'Connor, I have to go to work now. You should make friends with Poppy, and be good for Rhea.' She waited, watching him stop in his tracks and turn to face her. 'Come and say goodbye.' She held out her arms to him and after a moment's hesitation he came and gave her a hug and a kiss.

'I will, but she started it.' He looked up at Allison, his expression earnest. 'I want my soldier back.'

'Then you must ask Rhea to deal with it, instead of getting into a fight over your toys.'

Connor looked doubtful about that, his jaw firmly set, his shoulders going back, as though he was unwilling to pass up on his responsibilities, and Allison's heart gave a squeeze. He looked so much like his father at that moment, forthright, in control of himself, ready to deal with anything.

Connor looked at the medical bag she was holding and said, 'You going now? You going to help the poorly people?'

'That's right.'

He wound his arms around her as far as he could reach. 'Bye, Mummy.' His smile was angelic, as though butter wouldn't melt in his mouth, and Allison lightly ruffled his dark silky hair, her whole being filled with love for her troublesome offspring.

'Bye, sweetheart.'

She gave Poppy a cuddle and said goodbye to Rhea, hurrying out of the house a few moments later, the children's renewed shouts echoing in her ears. The tube station was just a short walk away, and she made the journey to the centre of London in quick time.

She wasn't sure what to expect when she arrived at the gallery. There were emergency vehicles parked all around, and police had cordoned off the area, keeping worried onlookers back behind taped lines. Allison showed her medical badge and an officer escorted her inside the building.

'They're working as fast as they can to get to some people who are trapped under the rubble,' he explained, 'and there are parts of the building that are still not safe, so you'll need to follow the directions of the officer in charge.'

'I will. How did it happen, do you know?' she asked.

He shook his head. 'It's not clear at the moment, but we do know that some renovations were carried out recently, and the thinking is that they might have had something to do with the collapse. It appears that, over the years, several alterations have been made to the fabric of the building, but we don't know yet whether any of them could have affected the load-bearing structures. At any rate, it's bad. A lot of the stuff that came down is heavy, and there are a number of casualties.'

It certainly looked horrendous, and there was noise all around, groans and cries for help, mixed with the tense voices of the people who were trying to get to those who were hurt. Allison could see piles of rubble, made up of wood, steel and plaster, along with lumps of concrete, lodged at precarious angles. Everything was covered in a layer of dust, and even the air was clogged with it. Firemen were working to remove some of the wreckage, moving carefully so as not to cause more damage to the people who were trapped underneath.

Allison covered her nose and mouth with her hand so she didn't breathe in the choking dust and spoke to the man who was co-ordinating operations.

'We've managed to get some of the injured people out of the way of immediate danger,' he told her, 'and we've taken them to one side so that they can be treated initially.' He gestured towards a pillared archway, where things looked relatively safe. 'Dr Melbourne—James—is doing triage, and he'll tell you where you're needed.'

Allison hurried over there and spent the next hour going from one patient to another, giving oxygen and pain medication, stemming wounds and splinting fractures. At one point she straightened up from a kneeling position and stretched, easing the knotted muscles of her back, and took a look around.

Over at the far side of the gallery a mountain of debris was still in place and the fire crew had brought in lifting gear to try to move it. A man, wearing a jacket that marked him out as a doctor, was working his way over the rubble, moving carefully upwards, probing among the timbers and stopping from time to time in order to listen for any sound that might be coming from inside the mound.

Watching him, Allison's eyes widened and her heart began to thud heavily. Wasn't that someone she knew? Her breath caught in her throat. How could she mistake that tall figure?

It had been several long years since she had last seen him, but there was no mistaking that assured stance, or that measured way he had of looking at things. He was a man who would always stand out in a crowd. He was the one you would go to instinctively when you were in trouble, when you needed someone who could take charge.

Her mouth was suddenly dry. At the back of

her mind she had convinced herself that this day would not come, and that she would never see him again. She had been so sure that Taylor would change his mind about the new job, or that something would crop up to keep him in Hampshire—an enticing promotion, maybe, or at any rate an offer he couldn't refuse. Why would he abandon everything he had worked for to come and take over an A and E department just for a year?

The triage doctor called out, 'I need some help over here—a cardiac arrest.'

Allison hurried over to him and started compressions on the patient's chest while James charged the defibrillator. They worked together until the man's heart was shocked into a normal rhythm once more, and then Allison moved to one side while the paramedics carried the patient away to a waiting ambulance.

She was still unsettled by the knowledge that Taylor was there. She glanced towards the rubble. 'It looks as though something is going on over there, James,' she murmured. 'Do you think they've found someone?'

By now, Taylor was at the top of what had once been the mezzanine floor, and he was speaking to one of the fire crew. As she watched he began to ease himself down through a gap into the mass of broken timbers.

Allison sucked in a sharp breath. Surely he couldn't be going in there among all the fallen masonry?

'Yes, we believe there's a man trapped in there,' the doctor said. 'They heard him calling out earlier, but then he went quiet. It seems that the broken beams have formed a tent-like structure around him and that's keeping the worst of the masonry off him for the time being. Even so, it looks as though he has multiple injuries. The fire crew have been trying for some time to clear a way through to him, but it was too dangerous to allow anyone to get close enough to treat him.'

Allison frowned. 'But I just saw a doctor going in there.'

He winced. 'He must be crazy. If the concrete slabs collapse, we'll have an extra casualty on our hands.'

He marked off his patient's chart and excused

himself to go and talk to the paramedic about his patient's care. Allison made her way over to the place where the mezzanine floor had collapsed and managed to waylay one of the firemen.

'What's going on? Is there anything I can do to help?' she asked.

'I don't think so. We've managed to slide in some temporary supports, and we've rigged up a ladder to lie flat along the side of the heap so that we could slide a stretcher over there if necessary, but the whole thing is shaky. Everything might cave in if too much weight is placed on it. We're having to go very carefully.'

'But a doctor went in, didn't he?' Allison was alarmed at the thought of the masonry giving way. What was Taylor thinking of, putting his life in jeopardy?

'That's right, he did. He insisted on going in, because he said the man—his name's Matt, apparently—had crush injuries and it was important to get him out as quickly as possible.' He made a face. 'His patient is trapped by a steel and concrete strut, and we're doing what we can to prepare to lift it from him, but it's taking a while.

I think the doc is struggling a bit. He's trying to stem the bleeding and give the man lifesaving treatment, but there's not much room to move and he needs extra equipment—he says the man's ribs are broken and his breathing's impaired.'

'It sounds as though he has a collapsed lung.' Allison was thoughtful for a moment. 'I could get things to the doctor. I'm lighter than most of you, and I probably know what kind of help he needs.'

The fireman looked doubtful. 'We'd have to put a harness on you so that we could lift you to safety if things start to give way.'

'Then let's do that…as quickly as we can.'

Within minutes, she was ready. Holding on to her medical pack, she flattened herself against the ladder and eased her way upwards towards the gap in the wreckage. Peering down into the space where Matt lay injured, she shone a torch into the area.

She saw a man whose leg was wedged beneath a broken pillar, and Taylor was attending to him, working to save his life. He had managed to set up an intravenous line so that Matt would receive an infusion of vital saline. The fluid bag was suspended from a jutting slat of wood. Right now Taylor was applying a pad dressing to an open wound in Matt's arm.

'What can I do to help?' she asked softly.

Taylor looked up at her. He blinked, and she moved the torch so that the light was no longer shining in his eyes, but she caught his startled expression and knew that he was stunned to see her there.

'Allison?' His voice held a disbelieving note, as though he thought his eyes were deceiving him. 'I'd heard that you were in London, but...' He broke off and then added, 'You were called out?'

'Yes. Along with every other doctor who happened to be available.' There was a rumbling sound just then, like distant thunder, and her whole body tensed as something began to shift beneath her. The whole edifice was unstable and the knowledge that it might collapse made her feel sick and dizzy. She pressed her lips together and put her head down until the movement stopped.

When things had steadied, she opened her eyes and searched for the gap in the rubble once more. She was relieved to see that Taylor was still down there, crouched over his patient.

The man was groaning. 'Can't breathe,' he muttered. His eyes were frightened. 'I'm going to die, aren't I?'

'I'm not going to let that happen,' Taylor said. 'Bear with me.' He frowned, looking up at Allison. 'You shouldn't be here,' he said in a quiet tone. 'It's too dangerous. You should go. Get the fire crew to hoist up the medical equipment.'

She made a wry smile. 'It seems to me that you don't take your own advice, so why should I do what you say? Tell me what you need.'

He pressed his lips together, and his glance shifted over her. Perhaps he noticed the harness she was wearing but, whatever the reason, he obviously decided not to waste time arguing with her any more. 'A one-way valve—I can make one up from tubing and a container of water that can be sealed. He has a pneumothorax.'

'I have those things here, and some lignocaine for the anaesthetic.' She delved into her medical pack and passed the equipment to him, watching while he worked to reinflate the man's lung.

'We'll get you out of here, Matt,' he said in a low voice. 'Hang on in there.'

Little by little, the fire crew were removing debris from the heap that enclosed the injured man, and the escape route via the gap was gradually being widened. Allison helped them to slide a narrow stretcher through the opening, and then she tentatively made her way down into the tented structure, ready to assist. After a while, the team signalled that they were ready to attempt to lift the structure that was holding Matt down.

Taylor nodded, and eased himself out of the way within the cramped space so that they could work. He looked worried.

'When they move the beam,' he said, glancing at Allison, who was crouched beside him, 'we have to slide him onto the stretcher and strap him in place. He's stable for the moment, but he's floating in and out of consciousness all the while and things are going to be tricky when we manage to release the pressure from his leg. I'll give him a painkiller, but once the circulation starts up again, the pain will really start to kick in and his tissues will start to swell. When that happens there's always the danger of renal failure.'

'You've been giving him fluids—that should go some way to alleviate that problem.'

'That's true. I just hope that I've done enough so that we can save his leg.'

Things happened fairly quickly after that. As soon as the concrete was lifted, they worked together to slide Matt onto the stretcher. His groans became louder, but they concentrated on getting him out of there before everything around them could start to shift.

Taylor removed the fluid bag from the wooden slat and handed it to her. 'Will you keep this steady while I see to the oxygen mask and the bottle valve?'

She nodded. Between them, they eased him up far enough through the opening so that the waiting fire crew could take over. The men used the ladder to slide the patient down to safety, and then Taylor urged Allison to follow, lifting her up the last part of the way through the gap into the waiting hands of a fireman.

With his help, she clambered slowly over the

mound and flattened herself once more on the ladder so that she could make the descent back to ground level. As she slid down, though, the whole edifice started to move, tilting her at an acute angle, and she landed on the floor below with a heavy thump. A roaring started in her ears and wood, metal and concrete caved inwards, shooting a cloud of dust and debris into the air.

She lay there for a moment, thrown by her sudden descent, and shocked by the noise and chaos that was all around her. After a minute or two she lifted her head and then she began to cough, dust clouding her eyes and filling her mouth. Then, as her senses returned, she felt her pulse quicken as horror slowly filled her mind.

'Taylor,' she whispered. 'Taylor, where are you?' And what of the fire crew? What had happened to them? She tried to get up, but her head was reeling.

'Are you OK?' Strong hands reached for her, bringing her to her feet, and she stood for a moment, shakily trying to regain her balance. The man held on to her, his fingers curled around her arms, steadying her.

'I'm fine,' she said huskily. 'Really, I'm fine.' The man stood close to her, a calming presence, unmoving, waiting for her to collect herself. She looked up and saw that it was Taylor who was holding her, his grey eyes intent on her face, studying her as though he would search out any hint of anything that might be wrong.

A feeling of relief washed over her. 'You got away in time,' she said, and a slow breath of air left her lungs. 'What about the others…Matt, and the firemen?'

'Matt was already down. The rest of us were able to jump clear when the mass started to move.'

'I'm glad about that,' she said.

He nodded. Seeing that she was all right, he released her, and she felt a sudden pang of loss, a draught of cold air that wafted through her consciousness and made her tremble momentarily.

Taylor was looking at her all over again, taking her in from head to toe, and then his mouth tilted at the corners. 'You're covered in a film of dust,' he said, 'just as though you've walked through a flour factory.'

His comment had her shifting restlessly. Their

first meeting after all this time, and she had to look the worse for wear. She wished she could say the same about him, if only to even things up a bit, but for all his heroic manoeuvres amongst the wreckage, he was still in tantalisingly good form. She stared at him, trying to make sense of her chaotic emotions. He was shrugging out of his medic's jacket, and she guessed that he must be feeling the heat after being cooped up in a confined space for so long.

He was just as she remembered him, with that strong, angular jaw and those same brooding grey eyes that seemed to look into her soul. His hair was as black as night and cropped short. His casual clothes, dusky green chinos and pale-coloured shirt fitted him to perfection, so that she couldn't help but notice his broad shoulders and the long line of his legs. He was flat stomached, lean and muscular, and he made her blood heat up, just from looking at him.

'Shall we get out of here and get some fresh air?' he suggested, placing a hand on her elbow and ushering her towards the main door. He glanced around. 'There isn't much more we can do in here. All of the injured but one have been evacuated and they should be on their way to hospital any time now.'

'We don't have any choice but to leave them in the hands of the emergency teams, do we? I hope they all make it, especially Matt.'

He nodded. 'I told the paramedic that I'd go with him and see to it that he's all right on the journey.'

Outside in the open air, she blinked as the afternoon sunlight caught her unawares. A crowd had gathered, and instinctively she turned away, seeking quiet and solitude.

'There's a waiting area just behind where the ambulances are parked,' Taylor said. 'We can be peaceful there, away from prying eyes, while we wait for them to bring out the last patient.'

'Yes.' She felt strangely out of sorts now that the threat of immediate danger had passed. Her senses were numbed, and perhaps it was the shock of seeing him again that was making her react this way.

They walked to where Matt was being transferred to the waiting ambulance, and she took off her own jacket, shaking off the dust before laying it down on an iron railing. Delving in her bag for a moist wipe, she used it to clean her face and hands. Then she loosened the velvet scrunch from the back of her head and shook her hair free, running her hands through the pale golden strands until the dust fell away and her hair seemed to be silky and light to the touch once more.

Taylor watched her, his glance going slowly over her. 'Feel better now?' he asked.

'I think so.'

'You shouldn't have done what you did back there, you know,' he said. 'It was far too risky... But when all's said and done, you were great. You helped to save Matt's life.'

'Maybe, but so did you.' She looked at him. 'I didn't see you holding back, whatever the outcome might have been.'

But, then, he never had. He was always one to take control where necessary, wanting to make sure that things would turn out all right. Hadn't he done the same when she'd last seen him all those years ago?

Her mind drifted back to that fateful evening.

It had started out uneventfully enough. She and Rhea had gone for a pleasant evening out, she remembered, enjoying a meal at a quiet little country pub back home in Buckinghamshire. Rhea had wanted to tell her all about the new man she had taken up with, and everything had gone fine until Rhea's ex-boyfriend had come along in search of her.

He had never accepted that she hadn't wanted to see him any more, and he had been determined to cause trouble from the outset. The argument that had followed outside the pub had been unavoidable, and he'd dragged Rhea away by force, ignoring her protests. Allison had tried to intervene, anxious to help her friend out, but he had retaliated, threatening her, and she had been helpless to do anything to stop him.

Making up her mind to follow them, Allison discovered that it wasn't going to be possible. Her car tyres had been slashed, and it didn't take much guesswork to figure out who was responsible. She was virtually stranded, and everything that had happened had left her nerves shattered. It had started to snow, and now, because of the lateness of the hour, she couldn't get a taxi to come out at short notice.

Feeling cold, wet and miserable, and not knowing what to do for the best, she phoned her brother's one-time friend to see if he could help. Things had gone wrong between her brother and Taylor, but he was the only one who lived within a reasonable distance and she didn't know what else to do.

Taylor arrived just a short time later, her knight in shining armour. He was Rhea's knight, too, as it turned out, because when he heard what had happened he went in search of her, squaring up to her ex-boyfriend and sending him on his way. Then he dropped Rhea off at her house and set out to take Allison home.

She grimaced. Perhaps things would have turned out very differently if they had arrived there as planned.

'You look a little subdued,' Taylor said now, dragging her thoughts back to the present. 'I suppose that's not surprising, after what we've just been through. It seems an odd way for us to meet up after all this time, doesn't it?'

'Yes, you're right, it does.' She glanced at him. 'And it has been a long time since we've seen anything of each other.'

His expression was serious, his eyes dark and unreadable. 'Considering that we spent so much time together as teenagers, things turned out very differently from what we might have expected, didn't they?'

More so than he could possibly have imagined, she reflected wryly, but she wasn't about to let him in on her thoughts. Her mouth made an awkward shape. 'Perhaps that's so…but you had that offer of a post as registrar, and I went off to do my house-officer year. We've both moved on in the last few years.'

'I suppose we have.' He frowned. 'I heard that your mother died. I was sorry about that—it must have been a bad time for you and your brother. I tried to contact you, but you weren't living at your mother's house and you obviously didn't receive my letter, because it was returned to me. I had no idea where you were working by then.'

Her eyes widened a fraction. She hadn't realised that he had made the effort to keep in touch.

'I didn't know you had written to me. I wonder if a neighbour returned the letter by mistake, or perhaps it was the estate agent? The house was empty for a while when Mum went into hospital, and then we had an agent sort out the sale of the property.'

'I guess that must have been what happened.' He sent her a searching look. 'Of course, I wasn't sure that you wanted to know me any more. After all, you didn't stop to say goodbye. It was a very final, abrupt ending to our relationship.'

Warm colour washed over her cheekbones and she pressed her lips together, discomfited by the memory of that night. 'Things shouldn't have gone the way they did.'

'No? You didn't seem to be too concerned about that at the time.'

She sucked in a sharp breath. That was a low blow. Did she really deserve that kind of reaction from him? It seemed to her that everything that night had seemed to be out of her control.

'It was all a mistake,' she said. 'I wasn't thinking clearly.'

That was true enough. Snow had been falling

steadily, casting a blanket over the landscape, and she had been numb with cold. On their way home from Rhea's house, they had stopped to help a couple whose car had skidded on a patch of ice. The woman had had a concussion from a bang on her head, while the man had suffered cuts and bruises. By the time they had patched them up and helped them on their way, Allison had been shivering from the freezing weather and Taylor had wrapped her up in a blanket and driven her to his home.

'My place is nearer than yours,' he said. 'I think we'll get you warmed up and back on your feet before we go any further.'

And that, in the end, had been her undoing…because he'd sat her down and given her brandy to coax the heat back into her, holding her in his arms while she'd recovered, and he'd listened to her worries about her brother, and about her mother's failing health. He'd comforted her and made her feel warm and cherished, and all the while her head had become more and more muzzy from the alcohol, so that before she'd taken on board what she'd been getting into, they had been making love, and all her problems had seemed to disappear on a cloud of passion.

Of course, they came back in full force when she woke up the next morning with a fogged brain and discovered that she was still in his house…in his bed. Taylor was still sleeping as she quickly dressed and called for a taxi.

Her mind was reeling. It had all been a dreadful mistake. She had never meant to get involved with him in that way. She didn't go in for one-night stands and it horrified her to know that she had let her feelings run away with her this one time.

He had been her brother's friend from their school days, and it was inevitable that she would grow close to him. She had admired and respected Taylor, had hungered after him from afar, but there was never going to be any future for her with him, she had known that all along. He had always been career orientated, always on the move, and he wasn't in the market for commitment.

Then he and Nick had a disagreement, a falling-out over something that affected Nick's business enterprise, and he moved on, even from that once solid friendship.

'You might not have been thinking clearly at the time,' Taylor said now, 'but surely the next morning there was at least some time for reflection? I was surprised, to say the least, to find that you had gone.'

'I left you a note,' she murmured. 'I didn't know you were going away that very day. You didn't tell me, and I only found out later on.'

She frowned as the paramedic signalled to him that they were ready to move off with the ambulance and his patient. 'In the back of my mind, I suppose I thought we might bump into one another at some point in the future.'

His mouth twisted. 'Oh, yes,' he said. 'I found your brief message.' He moved towards the ambulance. 'Strange that it should be five years before we came across one another once more, isn't it?'

She didn't answer him. It was more than simple reticence that had kept her from staying in touch. She had a lasting reminder of that evening they had spent together. Her son,

Connor, shaped her every thought and deed, and above all she had determined to keep him safe and secure. Better to have no father at all than one who was always on the move.

'I have to go,' Taylor said, 'but I guess we'll be seeing each other again fairly soon.' He flicked a glance at her name badge. 'Dr Allison Matthews, King's Bridge Hospital.' His mouth made a wry slant. 'I'm going to be working there, too, so it looks very much as though we'll be seeing quite a bit of each other, one way or another, over the next few months.'

He frowned. 'I wonder how that will work out…especially as it seems that I'm going to be your new boss.'

CHAPTER TWO

CONNOR gazed at the open green space behind the primary school, taking in the cluster of trees and the leaves that fluttered gently in the light breeze.

'Can we go to the park after school?' He skipped along beside Allison, heading through the school gates and jumping into the air every now and then out of sheer exuberance.

'We'll see.' Allison wasn't going to commit herself. 'It all depends whether or not you can stay out of trouble. You know, your teacher said you weren't really paying attention to her yesterday, and you keep squabbling with your friends. What's that all about?'

Connor stopped skipping and shrugged, his lips jutting in a rebellious fashion. 'They 'noy me,' he said. 'They push me when I'm having a think, so

I push them back.' He looked up at her, spreading his arms wide. 'What am I s'pposed to do?'

Allison hid a wry smile. 'Just try talking to them,' she said. 'Use your voice instead of your hands.'

He blinked, giving that some thought, and then he gave her a sideways glance, his mouth curving sweetly. 'I'll be good,' he promised. 'So can we go to the park?'

'Perhaps…if you remember what I said.'

She gave him a hug and a kiss and watched him run into his classroom. He greeted his friends without a care in the world, and she turned away, heading for the street. It wasn't like him to misbehave, and so far there had only been a few instances, but they were enough to make her a little concerned. If the teacher had commented on his behaviour, then there might be a problem brewing.

Allison frowned, and hurriedly walked the half a mile or so to the tube station. It was a beautiful spring morning, and the scent of blossom filled the air. She breathed it in and tried to relax…not an easy thing to do, under the

circumstances. Today was going to be a challenge, if only because Taylor would be on duty
at the hospital, and in order to cope with that she
needed all her wits about her. Still, she was
scheduled to be on call to go out with the rapid
response unit today, so perhaps she would be
able to avoid him.

As things turned out, he wasn't anywhere to
be seen when she arrived in A and E. 'Dr
Briscoe is with a patient in the resuscitation
bay,' Sarah, the specialist nurse, told her. 'We've
been kept pretty busy up to now, but he seems
to be very much on the ball. It looks as though
he takes everything in his stride.' She smiled.
'Somehow I think we're going to like having
him around.'

Allison wasn't at all sure about that. His
presence here had opened up all sorts of uncer-
tainties for her…most of all, the worry of not
knowing what to tell him regarding Connor.

It was a problem she had thought about end-
lessly these last few years. For a long time, after
she had first discovered that she was carrying
Taylor's child, she had thought about calling

him to tell him the news, but always, at the last minute, she had held back. She had been unwell, and at first there had been the danger of a miscarriage, the uncertainty of whether she would be able to carry the baby to full term, and what would it have served to alert him unnecessarily?

She was still undecided about what to do. Perhaps, for the time being, she would do best to steer clear of the issue altogether.

'Will you take a look at a patient in the trauma room?' Sarah asked some time later. 'I think he must have been involved in a fight last night because there's bruising around his face, and from the look of his X-rays he has several rib fractures. The registrar ordered a CT scan before he went off duty, and we have the results of that now. It looks as though there's a haematoma.'

'Of course.' Allison went along to assess the patient, and confirmed Sarah's diagnosis.

'There's a build-up of blood in the wall of your chest,' she told the man. 'That's making it difficult for you to breathe, so we need to put in a tube and drain it for you. We'll make sure that you have something to relieve the pain, and we'll admit you to the observation ward for a time, until we feel that you're well enough to go home.'

She glanced at the patient. He was in a sorry state, and she couldn't help wondering how the other man in the fight had fared. Something about him stopped her from asking, though, and maybe it was because there was a familiar look about him. He reminded her very much of Steve, Rhea's ex-boyfriend, mainly because he had the same craggy features and was thick set.

'Are you about finished in here?' Taylor's deep voice intruded on her thoughts a short time later, as she finished setting the drainage tube in place. He pulled the curtain of the cubicle to one side and walked in.

She glanced at him, her throat going dry. He was wearing a cool-looking mid-blue shirt and dark trousers that clung to his hips and hinted at strong, muscled thighs. 'Yes. I was just about to hand over to Sarah so that she can dress the wound. Why? Did you need me for something?'

He nodded. 'We've had a callout to a fire at a

bus depot on the west side of London, near Ealing. You're on the rota to work with the response team, aren't you? We need to go now.'

Allison's chest constricted. She hadn't missed the fact that he had said, '*We* need to go.' She nodded briefly and sent her patient a quick look. 'You should begin to feel a little more comfortable soon,' she said. 'Sarah will take care of you from this point, so if you have any concerns or queries, just ask.'

The man made an attempt at a smile. 'Thanks, darling.'

Allison felt a small shiver run through her. That was what Steve used to say. Everyone had been 'darling' or 'sweetheart', and there was nothing wrong with that, it was an endearment, except that when Steve had said it, he had always managed to make her feel uncomfortable. Perhaps it had been because, behind the honeyed words, there had always been the simmering threat of violence.

Allison walked with Taylor to the locker room where her jacket and medical pack were stored. 'How is it that you're coming out with the response unit?' she asked. 'I thought Greg was the doctor in charge of that.'

'He is, but I want to see how the unit works.' He sent her an oblique glance. 'Does it bother you that I'll be going with you?' His eyes said that he was very well aware that it did.

She shook her head, clamping her lips together. 'No, not really,' she said, but it was an outright lie, and he probably recognised that. Just knowing that he was nearby and that they would be in each other's company day after day was already having a disastrous effect on her nervous system.

In fact, she wouldn't have been surprised to learn that he had arranged to be part of the response team deliberately, just so that they would have to work together. Was he paying her back for walking out on him?

He didn't pursue the matter any further. 'You looked preoccupied when I came to find you just then,' he murmured. 'Was your patient giving you problems?'

'No. It was just that he reminded me so much of Steve, Rhea's ex. I couldn't help but think back to how much trouble he used to cause her.'

He frowned. 'But that's all over with now, isn't it? She married someone else and had a child, or so I heard.'

'Yes, she did, but the marriage didn't work out, and I don't know that Steve ever gave up on stalking her. She's had to move house several times in the last few years just to keep one step ahead of him.'

By now they had collected their gear and they hurried out to the waiting ambulance car. Taylor slid behind the wheel and started up the engine.

'I didn't know that…but I seem to have missed out on quite a lot of the news while I've been working down in Hampshire. What else has happened while I've been away? I see you qualified as an A and E doctor but, then, I always knew you would. It was either that or paediatrics, with you.'

Her heart wrenched. Paediatrics had been crossed off her list once she had given birth to her son. Holding him in her arms, she had known that she wouldn't be able to cope with the stress of treating sick children every day.

He was waiting for an answer as to what had

been happening, and she could have used that opportunity to say to him, 'When you left, I discovered that I was pregnant. I gave birth to your son.' But the words stuck in her throat and her pulse began to hammer. Of course it was the wrong time to say any of that.

Instead, she told him, 'After we sold Mum's house, I moved into a property in Kilburn, and Nick used his part of the proceeds to set up in business once more in a place just outside the City.' It was a sore point, the fact that her brother had had to start over, and she wondered how Taylor would react to that comment. Wasn't he partly to blame for her brother's troubles?

His eyes narrowed, but other than that he didn't respond, except to ask, 'Is he still in partnership with Ben?'

She nodded. 'Of course. Why wouldn't he be? They're both skilled craftsmen, and they work well together.' Her brother's bespoke furniture business was still in its infancy, but she had every faith in him to make it succeed this time around.

They were travelling as fast as traffic restrictions allowed, passing through the residential suburbs of West London, and Taylor followed a route by the Grand Union Canal. Through the trees Allison caught a glimpse of colourful barges moving slowly on the water. It was a leisurely kind of existence that seemed incongruous with the fast pace of London life, but it was something she longed to experience.

'I'm taking a short cut,' he told her. 'I used to come out here with my sister, when we were younger, to wander through Perivale Wood. They open it up to the public when the bluebells are in full bloom, but otherwise it's kept as a nature reserve for members or for groups of school children to visit. There are nature trails to follow, and we used to like looking at the ponds and streams. Claire had a thing for wildlife. She couldn't get enough of trips out.'

'Yes, I remember that.' Allison glanced at the distant stretch of trees and green open space. 'She has children now, doesn't she? Do they get to share in her love of nature?'

He gave a short laugh. 'I expect so, from time to time, but you have to go carefully with those two boys. Trouble seems to be their middle name and you might be able to take them out somewhere, but you wouldn't necessarily want to take them back there again.'

Allison smiled wryly. His comments made her forget for the moment that they were headed out to the site of an accident, but he brought her back to reality soon enough.

'We're here.' He pulled up some distance from the bus depot, and even from here they could see and smell the cloying thick black smoke that billowed into the air. 'This is about as close as we can get, I think.'

'How did the fire come about, do you know?'

'I don't think they have any real idea yet, but there was some talk of an engine catching fire and igniting the blaze elsewhere. I imagine there will be an enquiry into the cause.'

They stepped out of the car and began to hurry towards the depot. Allison could see that two of the buses were on fire, but as they approached there was a sudden explosion and the sound of breaking glass ripped through the air. In an instant Taylor had pulled her to one side, holding her back against a wall and sheltering her with his tall frame.

She was stunned by the force of the explosion, and shocked by the roaring sound of the fire, mixed with the noise of shattered fragments falling to the ground. Most of all she was aware of Taylor's strong body against hers, his jaw lightly grazing her cheek so that she registered the slight roughness of his skin as he bent his head to protect her. Her breasts were crushed against the hard wall of his chest, and she could feel the warmth emanating from him. She felt the heavy thud of his heartbeat as he leaned into her, keeping her from harm.

Being this close to him made her senses spin. It called to mind how it had been that night so long ago when he had held her in his arms, and the heat rose in her, stifling her common sense and making her want what could not possibly be. It was madness to think that their coming together back then had been anything more than a momentary lapse.

After a while he eased himself away from her,

hesitating before he glanced around. Smoke drifted around them, carried on the air by a gust of wind. 'I think the explosions have stopped for the moment,' he said in a gruff, thickened voice. 'There must have been a build-up of intense heat to cause the blow-out, but it looks as though the firemen are moving in with foam spray. Perhaps we can safely get to our patients now.'

Had he been at all affected by their unexpected closeness? Allison glanced at him. He seemed to be very much his usual self now, and it must have simply been the smoke in the atmosphere that had roughened his voice. She wasn't sure quite how she felt about him recovering so easily, but she decided to take her lead from him. It was important that she should bring her mind back on track. After all, they had a job to do.

Allison went with him to where the ambulance crew was gathered. A young woman was sitting on a bench by a wall, being attended to by a paramedic as she struggled to breathe, and near to her there was a man who was lying down on an ambulance trolley. He was suffering from obvious burns to his hands, and there was an oxygen mask in place over his nose and mouth. He looked to be in a bad way.

The second paramedic was looking after the man, dressing his burns, and he said quietly, 'This is Jacob. He was in the driver's cab when the engine caught fire and I'm concerned about his condition. Apart from the burns, he's suffering from smoke inhalation, and I'm afraid that some of the fumes in the depot must be toxic. His consciousness level is falling and his heart rhythm has been affected.'

'I'll try to intubate him,' Taylor said, looking grim. 'The sooner we can get an airway into him the better.'

The paramedic made way for him and Taylor introduced himself to the patient. 'Jacob, I'm Dr Briscoe. Can you hear me? How are you doing?' Allison guessed that he was looking for a response so that he could assess the man's level of consciousness.

Jacob mumbled something, but the words were indistinct, and Taylor said quickly, 'It's all right…we're going to look after you. I just need to look down your throat for a moment.' He worked swiftly after that, grimacing as he said to Allison, 'The throat tissues are swelling up. This is going to be tricky.'

At the second attempt he managed to insert the tube, and the paramedic hurried to hook Jacob up to an oxygen supply. Allison set up an intra-venous line so that they could give him resusci-tating fluids, and then, at a shout from the paramedic nearby, she handed over to Taylor and went to take a look at the young woman.

'Her name is Tracey,' the man who was helping her said. 'She's eight months pregnant and suffering from asthma. She's used her sal-butamol inhaler, but it doesn't seem to be working.' As he spoke, the woman started to slip sideways, and he caught her, supporting her and laying her down along the bench.

'She's not with us,' Allison said in alarm, feeling for her pulse. 'I'm going to give her a shot of epinephrine.' She used an auto-injector, but it didn't cause the reaction she hoped for and she and the paramedic started immediate cardiopulmonary resuscitation. Taylor came to assist, and between them they managed to put in an airway and shock the heart back to a sinus rhythm.

'Let's get both patients into the ambulance,' Taylor said. 'You go with them to the hospital, and I'll follow in the car.'

Allison nodded agreement. She was worried about the woman, but the man wasn't doing well, either, and her heart was in her mouth on the journey back to King's Bridge.

Taylor met up with them in the ambulance bay a few minutes after they got back to the hospital. 'Has there been any change?' he asked.

'Tracey's pulse is thready,' Allison told him, as they hurried into A and E, 'and the foetal heart rate is slow. I'm worried that neither of them is receiving enough oxygen. We're going to have to do an emergency Caesarean, or we risk losing both of them.'

'Did you call ahead to have the anaesthetist standing by?'

'Yes, I did that. I asked for a team to make themselves ready, but they said all the theatres are occupied right now.' She grimaced. 'As to

Jacob, I'm concerned about his cardiovascular symptoms.'

'We'll get some lab tests done,' Taylor said, 'but I expect in Jacob's case the result will show cyanide poisoning along with carbon monoxide. I thought I detected a smell of bitter almonds in the air when we were at the depot. Cyanide gas is given off when things like plastics, wool and rubber are burned and it can have a disastrous effect on the nervous or cardiovascular systems.'

He turned to the nurse who had come to assist. 'Take him into the resuscitation bay for the time being. Keep him on high-flow oxygen and monitor his heart rhythm, pulse and blood pressure while we wait for the results,' he said. To Allison, he added, 'Let's get Tracey into the treatment room. We need to get her prepped for a Caesarean. We'll do it here. We don't have time to get her up to Theatre anyway. Her oxygen level is falling dangerously low.'

It was a nerve-racking time for all of them. Sarah called once more for the obstetrician and the paediatrician to come down to A and E and be ready to assist, and as soon as the anaesthetist had made sure that the epidural injection was working properly to numb the area, Taylor started the procedure. The mother-to-be was weakening fast, and there was no time to waste.

'I'm going to make a small incision across the bikini line,' he said, looking at Tracey to see if there was any response. 'You might feel a slight pulling sensation, but you won't feel any pain.' Tracey didn't answer, and he went to work swiftly, skilfully, so that within a very short time he had cut into the uterus and was ready to bring the baby into the world.

'It's a boy,' Taylor said, a minute or so later, his tone flat, 'but he doesn't seem to be in good shape.'

Allison could see straight away that there was a problem. The infant wasn't making a sound. He was limp and unmoving, and she felt her heart contract. Were they too late?

Taylor clamped and cut the cord, then handed the baby to her, before turning his attention back to the mother.

Allison hurried to one side of the room to examine the infant. 'He isn't breathing,' she told

Sarah. 'I'll have to apply suction to clean out his mouth and nose.' Once she had done that, she checked again to see if he was breathing and then shook her head. Sarah looked distressed, but quickly fetched an oxygen mask.

Allison started chest compressions on the infant, circling her hands around him so that her thumbs met over his breastbone. 'There's still no response,' she whispered after a minute. 'I'll intubate and give him intravenous epinephrine and maybe check for acidosis. I might need to give him bicarbonate.'

Things looked bad, but Allison went on with her efforts and after a while the baby's abdomen made a small movement and his chest wall rose slightly. Sarah made a choking sound. 'He's breathing,' she said, her mouth breaking into a smile. 'You've brought him back.'

'*We've* brought him back,' Allison said, her own tension slipping away. 'He's beginning to pink up nicely, isn't he?' She glanced to where Taylor was still working to bring the mother's breathing under control, and he returned her gaze, his grey eyes showing a gleam of satisfaction.

The paediatrician arrived soon after that, and Allison left the baby in her care while she went to see how the mother was doing.

'She's a little better,' Taylor said in a low voice. 'Once the baby was delivered, the pressure on her blood vessels was relieved. The inferior vena cava decompressed and with that her circulation started to improve. She isn't out of the woods yet, though. We need to add a bronchodilator to the nebuliser to help with her breathing and we have to monitor the corticosteroid dosage. That baby won't have a mother unless we can put an end to this asthma attack.'

She worked with him for the next hour, until they had done all they could to stabilise Tracey's condition, and then Taylor went to check on the bus driver, who was still in dire straits.

'I'll come with you,' Allison said, but he stopped her.

'No. You should go and take a break. I'll deal with this. We've been on the go all day and it's coming up to the end of your shift. You look drained, and I don't recall you having taken a break yet, apart from a quick five minutes you managed to snatch earlier on.'

She frowned. How had he known about that? How could he have managed to keep an eye on her movements while he'd been busy tending to his patients? Every time she had looked for him that morning, he had been occupied elsewhere, dealing with some trauma or other, and yet it seemed that he had somehow kept tabs on everyone. This afternoon, even though they had been taking care of the bus-depot patients, he had been aware of everyone's individual assignment.

'I need to keep watch on the rest of my patients,' she protested. 'The man with the broken ribs was admitted to the observation ward, and I have someone else waiting for results of a liver biopsy.' Besides, she was anxious to see how the driver was doing.

'The registrar will see to that.' His tone was firm, brooking no argument. 'He's back from his meeting, so you've no worries there.'

She made a face. It was no wonder he had achieved the exalted position of consultant while he was still in his mid-thirties. He must have eyes in the back of his head, as well as the ability to supervise several tasks at one time.

His comment about not taking a break worked both ways, though. He had been monitoring his patients constantly, and she hadn't noticed him pause to swallow as much as a sip of coffee. Even so, he wasn't showing any signs of fatigue. He was still straight-backed, driven and totally in command of himself.

She gave in, going along to the rest room to help herself to coffee and a sandwich. It was true enough that she was beginning to feel the strain. Not only did she have more patients to attend to but Connor was expecting her to take him to the park later on, and she didn't want to let him down. She needed to revitalise herself, though, before she even contemplated doing that.

Allison stayed in the room long enough to splash water on her face and run a brush through her long, fair hair. Then, feeling refreshed, she took a deep breath and stepped back into the fray once more. She headed for the patients' waiting room.

When they weren't coping with life-or-death

situations, there were always the everyday emergencies to be dealt with. The waiting room was full of a seemingly endless number of people, and she took a chart from off the top of the pile and went to call her next patient.

'Mrs Westerby?'

A woman in her thirties stood up and walked towards Allison, her wrist supported by a make-shift sling. She had a child with her, a little boy, around the same age as Connor. A minute ago he had been sitting next to her, swinging his legs to and fro, but now he jumped up, sending his chair skidding across the floor.

Allison winced at the screeching sound it made. The noise became louder as the child pushed it back into position. When he had finished what he was doing, she directed the woman along the corridor towards the treatment bay and suggested that she sit down. The boy came with them, standing next to his mother and looking around with interest.

Allison put the X-ray film into the light box. 'You've broken a bone in your wrist,' she said, pointing out the line of the fracture. 'It's a straightforward one, so we'll just need to put a cast on that for you. I'll give you a prescription for some painkillers, as well.' She gave the woman a brief smile. 'Excuse me for a moment while I go and see if I can find a nurse to prepare the cast for me.'

She went out into the main treatment area and signalled to Sarah to come over to the treatment bay. 'Would you put Mrs Westbury's wrist in a cast for me?' she asked, and Sarah nodded, going off to fetch what she needed.

'The coffee-break must have done you some good,' Taylor said, glancing at Allison as he passed by on his way to the central desk. 'You're looking fresh as a daisy, and the sparkle's back in your eyes.'

'Is it?' Colour washed into her cheeks.

'Oh, yes.' He looked her over, his gaze taking in the smooth line of her cotton top where it clung to her curves and noting the gentle swell where her skirt lightly skimmed her hips. 'Definitely.'

He moved towards her, coming closer, and she wondered what was causing the faint upward tilt of his mouth. She sent him a cautious glance, trying to fathom his mood, but he seemed to be distracted. He was looking at the silky sweep of her hair where it lightly brushed her shoulders.

'You always did have hair that looked like spun gold,' he murmured, reaching out a hand as though to playfully tweak a wayward strand, 'and there were always those mischievous curls that refused to conform.'

'Really?' Her green gaze was sceptical. 'I wasn't aware that you had ever noticed. I don't recall you ever paying me all that much attention in the past.'

'You're wrong,' he murmured. 'Besides, you can't have forgotten that winter's night back home, can you? I seem to remember paying you a whole lot of attention back then.'

His smoky-grey glance wandered over her and a wave of heat ran through her from head to toe. He was doing this to unnerve her, wasn't he?

'That was just the once,' she said, driven to make things clear. 'Everything was running way out of hand, and neither of us was thinking straight. I was still in a state over what had happened, with Rhea being dragged away, and having to deal with her ex, and then you came along and found me when I was vulnerable. It all seemed to tip out of control after that.'

His mouth lifted at the corners in a wry smile. 'So it was all just a momentary lapse…is that what you're trying to say?'

'Maybe.' She looked at him, determined to keep her gaze steady. 'Yes, I think it is.'

He laughed softly. 'A very memorable one, though, don't you think? It's all still very vivid in my mind.'

She pulled in a quick breath and told herself that she wasn't going to rise to his teasing. He was in a good frame of mind, though, and she was almost tempted to open up to him. Perhaps she could say, 'There's something important that I need to tell you. Could we take five minutes and have a talk?'

He cut in before she had time to get to grips with the issue. 'I suppose you'll be off home in a while,' he murmured. 'Do you have plans for the evening?'

'I—Yes, actually, I do. I promised that I would meet up with someone. He'll be waiting for me.'

He frowned, and the breath constricted in her lungs. What would his reaction be if she were to tell him that she was taking her son to play on the swings in the park? Ought she to tell him?

Before she could come to a decision one way or the other, Taylor's attention was distracted. Her patient's young son must have discovered that there were other, more exciting avenues to be explored rather than simply waiting around with his mother. The child put his foot onto the treatment trolley that Sarah had brought in, and he pushed off with it, using it like a scooter, riding along the length of the room.

'Ryan, come back here,' his mother said sharply, but by now he was out of earshot.

Taylor acted swiftly. He went after him, grabbing hold of the trolley and holding on to the boy in order to stop him from tumbling. 'I know it seems like fun, but you can't do that in here,' he told the child in a low voice. 'You might bump into someone and hurt them. There are a lot of poorly people in here.'

'Let go of me.' The boy aimed a sharp kick at Taylor's shin. 'Put me down.'

'I will, just as soon as you're back with your mother.' Taylor railroaded him back to the treatment bay and sat him down on a bed. 'Is there anyone with you who can watch over him while you're with the nurse?' he asked the woman.

She nodded. 'Yes, I'm sorry. My husband went off to get a drink from the machine. He should be along at any minute.'

'That's OK. Don't worry about it.' He replaced the trolley and handed the boy a pad and pencil, which he took from off the central desk. 'See if you can draw a scooter,' he said, giving him a long look.

The boy scowled at him, and Taylor walked back to Allison. 'Thank heaven I don't have any children,' he said through gritted teeth. 'I'm not sure that I'd have the patience to deal with them day after day.'

Allison looked at him, trying to disguise her dismay. 'They can be a handful, I admit,' she said in mitigation, 'but there are compensations, surely? I mean, most people love their offspring to bits and just enjoy watching them as they go through all those growing stages.'

He gave a short laugh. 'Well, maybe you're right. I guess I'm just too focussed on my work at the moment. It's very important to me. It's taken a lot of effort for me to get where I am today, and yet I still feel there's so much to achieve. Children just don't figure in my grand scheme of things.'

He shrugged, moving his shoulders in a backward arc, as though easing the tension there. 'I'd better go and check on our bus driver,' he said.

Allison watched him turn away. So that was about as far as she was going to get in trying to tell him her news, wasn't it? The knowledge that she was keeping it from him weighed heavily on her shoulders, but what was she to do? He didn't want a family…he had said so outright, and there was never going to be a good time to let him know that it was too late, that he was already a father, was there?

CHAPTER THREE

'WOULD you sign off this chart for me?' Greg asked, handing a folder over to Taylor. 'All the tests have proved negative up to now, and I want to send the patient home.'

Taylor glanced at the paperwork and then wrote his name at the foot of the document, his penstrokes black and bold. He added a note, though, and said tautly, 'Make sure that you arrange a follow-up scan with Outpatients. It isn't urgent, but it's best to get one done within a couple of months, just to be on the safe side.'

'I'll do that.' Greg hesitated, and Allison, who was looking through files at the desk nearby, could see that he was a bit worried about something. That was unusual. Greg was a pleasant, easygoing capable man in all respects, and Allison always got on well with him.

He sent Taylor a quick look and added, 'Would it be all right with you if I were to swap shifts with Simon tomorrow? My wife has to go and look after her sick mother down in Sussex, and I feel that the least I can do is drive her down there tonight. I'll be back the day after tomorrow. I've cleared it with Simon, and he's happy to do that for me.'

Taylor frowned. 'Simon's a very junior doctor, and we could do with having someone more experienced on at the weekend. Have you asked Allison if she would consider changing with you? She might be a better choice.'

Greg looked uncomfortable. 'I don't really want to ask Allison. She has to be quite careful about sticking to her duty rota—domestic issues and so on.'

Taylor's frown deepened, and he cast a swift glance in Allison's direction. She stiffened. She could tell that his senses were on the alert, and things could be awkward if he were to start asking questions and delving deeper.

'Simon's very bright—he knows his stuff, and he has a good deal more knowledge than the average junior doctor.' Greg was at pains to make things right, and Taylor's gaze shifted back to him.

Although Allison hadn't asked anyone to keep quiet about the fact that she had a son, they were all aware that Taylor was an unknown entity so far, and not all bosses appreciated having a single mother on the staff.

It was a situation that could be fraught with problems where rotas and overtime and unaccustomed hours were concerned. Allison did her best to pull her weight, the same as everyone else, and she had made sure that arrangements were in place with Rhea in case she ever had to work late, but she was always conscious of Connor's need to have his mother with him whenever it was possible. He was very young, and he had to be her prime concern.

'I suppose it will be all right,' Taylor conceded, though he didn't look too happy about it. 'At least I'll be on duty for some of the time tomorrow.' He handed back the chart and started to turn away. 'I'll be in the office if anyone wants me. I need to look through the notes we made when we did the interviews for the specialist nurses. We have to set someone on as soon as we can.'

'OK. Thanks for that.' Greg watched him go, then glanced at Allison. 'Sorry about that. I didn't mean to cause you any bother.'

'That's all right.' Her brows drew together. 'He doesn't seem to be his usual self today, does he? He's been looking a bit grim around the mouth all morning, as though he's out of sorts for some reason. Do you think he's concerned about setting up the new minor injuries walk-in centre?'

'No, I think that's all going fairly well. We'll certainly find that it helps with our work here in A and E once it gets off the ground. It should lessen our load. I think he's making some good changes around the place, and it's a pity that he's only going to be around for a fairly short time. We could do with someone of his calibre on a permanent basis.'

Allison nodded. She had always been impressed by Taylor's qualities of leadership, and the way he always managed to get things done against the odds. He was a man that you could respect. She recognised that even though she had her own deep-seated reservations about getting too close to him. Somehow she felt that if that were to happen, she could end up getting hurt. 'He certainly seems to know what he's doing.'

Greg smiled. 'Actually, I think the root cause of his trouble today is that he looked after his young nephews last night while his sister and her husband went out to celebrate their wedding anniversary. From what I heard, he stayed overnight at their house, while the parents enjoyed a night in a hotel. He must have had to get the children ready for school this morning, and I don't think it can have gone very well. He was looking a bit frazzled first thing, I thought.' He gave her a sideways glance. 'I expect you know all about that, having to deal with a four-year-old every day.'

'Oh, I do.' She gave a heartfelt sigh. 'There's always something that isn't right…either I've put out the wrong T-shirt, or he'll decide to take against his school trousers for some reason. Believe me, Connor can be really sweet, an absolute angel, but on other days he's a proper little crosspatch.'

She grimaced. 'This morning his problem was all about socks. They were too cold, he said, and he was so tetchy about it that I had to fit them, one at a time, over the end of the hairdryer and blow warm air into them before he was satisfied.' She shook her head. 'I couldn't believe that I was actually doing it, but it was either that or arrive at nursery school half an hour late.'

Greg laughed. 'I'd love to be a fly on the wall in your house in the mornings.' Then he sobered a fraction, and said, 'I wonder how Taylor coped with two of them—though his sister's boys are a little older than Connor...six and seven years, I think he said.'

'That sounds about right. When I last saw the family back in Buckinghamshire some five years ago, the boys were barely at the toddling stage.'

Sarah came over to them just then, and they were immediately on the alert. 'We have incoming patients,' she said. 'A road traffic accident. I'll go and tell Taylor.'

They were all kept busy for the next couple of

hours, but when the rush died down and there was finally time to take a break, Allison decided to go over to the maternity ward to see how the patient from the bus depot was getting along. It had been a few days since she had been admitted, but Allison had kept tabs on her progress, and she wanted to see whether the baby had suffered any ill effects.

'Hi, it's good to see you,' Tracey said, smiling as Allison put her head around the door of her room and peered inside. 'Come on in. I was just trying to freshen up ready for my husband's visit. The nurse has taken my baby to the nursery for a while to give him a check-up.'

'I won't stay, then, if your husband is coming in. How are you feeling?'

'Much better, thanks. My throat's still a bit uncomfortable from when the tube was in, but it helped to save my life, so I'm not complaining.' She looked at Allison directly. 'Thanks for everything that you did. I'm really grateful.'

'You're welcome. I'm just pleased to see you looking so well.'

Allison left her a few minutes later, and went

over to the nursery. When she arrived, though, she stopped in her tracks because Taylor was already there, bending over one of the cots. Seeing him there startled her, but perhaps he, too, had been worried about the baby's welfare.

She stood for a moment, watching him, not wanting to intrude, because there was something very special in what she was witnessing. In the end, though, she swallowed hard and then went over to him.

'Has the little fellow recovered from his ordeal?' she asked, and Taylor glanced up at her, his eyes widening a fraction.

'He's doing OK.'

He began to straighten up, but she saw that the infant was holding on to his finger, curling his fist around him and clinging on, and Taylor appeared to be reluctant to break that contact straight away. It was a sight that made her catch her breath. It was a wonderful thing to see, this strong, powerful man and the bond he had made with this tiny baby. It brought a lump to her throat.

She said softly, 'For a while I didn't think he was going to make it.'

His mouth made a crooked line. 'Neither did I, but it looks as though he's doing just fine now. His responses are all normal, and that's good to know.'

'Yes, it is.'

Allison gazed at the baby with affection, and Taylor finally managed to gently free himself. He straightened up and she was suddenly aware of how close they were to one another. He was standing so close to her that with the slightest movement she would have brushed against his shirtsleeve or felt the taut line of his thigh against hers. A wave of dizzying heat washed through her veins.

He sent her a contemplative glance, his grey eyes sweeping over her from head to toe, lingering for a moment on the shapeliness of her long legs, before moving upwards in quicksilver fashion to briefly dwell on the fullness of her mouth.

To Allison, it felt as though time had stood still, and for a while, as their glances met, the air crackled with electricity.

Then he pulled in a quick breath and stepped backwards, putting some distance between them. He seemed to give himself a mental shake before taking on the mantle of consultant once more. 'I should get back to A and E,' he said.

'Me, too.' She was almost relieved that the fleeting moment of tension that had passed between them had dissolved into nothingness. Her shoulders relaxed a fraction, but her heart was still thumping discordantly.

She followed him out of the door, and tried to turn her mind to everyday things. She asked him, 'Is there any news of the driver? I've been worried about him. I know you had everything under control, but cyanide poisoning sounds dreadful on top of everything else that happened to him, and I don't think I've come across it before.'

'We treat it with an antidote kit, made up of amyl and sodium nitrite, along with sodium thiosulphate. The chemicals combine with the cyanide to form a non-toxic substance which is then eliminated via the kidneys.' He paused, glancing at her. 'He's getting along all right, mainly because we managed to treat him on site and then get him to hospital in good time. The burns will take some time to heal, but at least the rest of his symptoms are under control.'

'I'm glad about that. As to treating him on site, it goes to show that the response unit is very worthwhile. It seems to work well, having doctors giving specialist medical treatment at an early stage.'

He sent her a quick look. 'It does…though it can play havoc with the staffing situation back here from time to time.' He frowned. 'Which reminds me—Greg seemed to imply that you might have to keep to a fairly rigid schedule as far as the duty rotas are concerned. Is there anything I need to know about? I sort of imagined that you were footloose and fancy-free these days, but perhaps I was wrong in assuming that? Maybe you don't live alone? Or has your father come back from the South Coast to be near you? I suppose that could cause problems for you.'

'No, he's still down there.' She passed the tip of her tongue over her dry lips. 'I do have to keep to a reasonable routine, though, and my weekends off are always precious.'

His gaze narrowed on her, and she guessed he was probably wondering whether she lived with someone.

She was wondering how she could let him know about Connor without causing a major upset in the workplace, but his pager went off just then, forestalling her. He paused to check the message, and stopped by the nurses' station to call for details, just as Allison's bleeper sounded.

'We've had a callout,' he said, throwing her a quick glance before writing down the address. 'It looks as though there's been an accident at an industrial estate in South West London. We need to head over there right away.'

Allison glanced at the address on the slip of paper and drew in a shocked gasp. 'That's where my brother has his workshop,' she said, a note of panic coming into her voice. 'Do you have any more details? Do you think it could be Nick's unit where the accident happened?'

Taylor shook his head. 'I wouldn't have thought so.' His grey eyes searched her face, assessing her with a measure of compassion, and she realised that she must have visibly paled.

'We're going to a tile warehouse—they store ceramics, glass and metal products. That doesn't sound like the sort of thing your brother's involved with, unless he's changed his type of business?'

She made an effort to pull herself together. 'No. He still makes furniture, but he moved into the bespoke market about a year ago. It's more exclusive than the work he did before, and it seems to be more in keeping with what he's always wanted to do. He designs home offices and all kinds of storage solutions. Ben's happier doing that, too.'

She hesitated. 'It took them a while to find these new premises, and the rent is a bit more than they wanted to pay, but at least they have room to expand. They had a slow start, getting the business off the ground, but I think it's beginning to take off at last.'

As they talked, they were on their way to the ambulance bay, stopping only to grab their packs, and let people know where they were going.

'I hope things turn out well for Nick, and for Ben,' Taylor said as he drove out of the City.

'Do you?' she asked. 'I wasn't so sure that you

had their interests at heart. They were established in their old premises until you intervened and they had to move on. Until then, I had thought you were Nick's friend.'

'I was.' He didn't respond to the element of reproach that threaded her tone, and that rattled her, because she wanted him to explain why everything had gone wrong. She had never understood how the two of them, who had been so close, could have let their friendship fall by the wayside.

'You had enough confidence in him to let him go ahead and renovate the old stable block, and you even bought some of his window-boxes and planters for your house in Buckinghamshire. I don't know what happened to make you turn against him. Did you find some fault with his work?'

His mouth straightened. 'That wasn't ever a problem. You must know that...after all, you invested some of your own money in the business, didn't you?'

'I had faith in him. I still do. I'm just not sure why you lost confidence in him.'

'Perhaps you should ask Nick to explain that.'

Allison's brows made a straight line. 'He doesn't know the reason.'

'I doubt that's true.' He turned his attention to the road ahead. They were approaching the Putney Bridge, crossing over the River Thames, and Allison looked out of the window to see the tranquil embankment and a line of trees in the distance.

Taylor briefly followed the direction of her gaze. 'That's where the annual Oxford and Cambridge boat race starts,' he said, and she wondered if he was making a deliberate change of tack. 'Have you ever watched the race from the bank?'

It was becoming clear to her that she was going to get nowhere if she tried to pursue the reasons behind the men's disagreement. 'No, I haven't, but I suppose I might one day, now that I'm settled in London.'

She didn't make any further comment. She was still put out by his unwillingness to enlighten her, and deep down she was worried in case the incident they were attending might have any repercussions for her brother.

'You didn't say what happened at the unit

we're heading for,' she remarked now. 'It isn't another fire, is it?'

'No. Apparently a forklift truck driver was trying to move a load of boxed tiles when he suddenly collapsed. It sounds as though the truck careered into someone who was in the loading bay at the time, but I don't know the extent of the injuries as yet.'

It didn't sound as though it was going to be anything very pleasant, and Allison tried to prepare herself for whatever they might find.

They passed by St George's Park, a green oasis in the middle of a built-up area, bordered by a river to the east, and she caught a glimpse of tennis courts through the trees. She had brought Connor here one day after they had been to visit her brother, and he had run about excitedly exploring the children's playground and exclaiming in delight when they'd seen the animals in the pets' corner.

'This is it,' Taylor said a minute or two later. 'Let's see what we have to deal with.'

They hurried past the ambulance that was parked in the forecourt and went into the red-brick building. The warehouse was in chaos, with tumbled boxes littering the floor and smashed tiles spilling out from them, covering the floor with shards of pottery and mirrored glass.

A paramedic quickly outlined what had happened. 'We have two injured men. One of them saw that there was a problem with the driver of the forklift, and he went to see if he could do anything to help. Unfortunately, the driver collapsed, and must have fallen against a mechanism that caused part of the truck to swivel, so that the load forks trapped the other man between the truck and the boxes. We've managed to free him, and he's fully conscious. There are no signs of any external wounds, but he's shocked and complaining of abdominal pain.'

'Will you go and take a look at him, Allison, while I see to the driver?' Taylor asked.

She nodded. The driver, a man in his fifties, didn't appear to be in a very good state, and she heard the paramedic say, 'He's conscious, but confused, and he's having some problems with his speech. There's also some weakness in his limbs. His blood pressure is high, too.'

Her own patient appeared to be lucid enough, but his blood pressure was low, along with his heart rate, and she was concerned that he might have suffered internal injuries of some sort.

'Hello, James. I'm Dr Matthews. I just want to examine you to see if there's any damage to your abdomen, if that's all right with you?'

He nodded and said through gritted teeth, 'Just don't press too hard. It hurts like—well, it hurts, OK?'

She nodded. 'I'll be careful.'

When she had finished her examination, she was more concerned than ever that all wasn't well. She decided to put in an intravenous line, so that she could give James painkilling medication and administer saline. He looked as though he was about to pass out with the pain, and it was becoming obvious that his condition was deteriorating. She wasn't at all sure that they would get to the hospital before he lost consciousness.

'What's the verdict?' Taylor asked, coming over to her.

'I think there's a build-up of blood in the

abdomen,' she said in a low voice, 'and I'm afraid that he might have ruptured his intestine. If that has happened, he's in trouble. I'm worried that he might go into shock and his circulation will close down.'

'Then we need to alert a surgeon, and make sure that there's a theatre on standby. You'd better start him on prophylactic antibiotics and be ready to resuscitate him if necessary.' He looked at her steadily. 'Are you prepared for that, or do you want me to go in the ambulance in your place? You haven't seemed to be quite yourself today.'

'No, I'll manage.' Perhaps he thought she was still on edge about her brother, but that didn't mean that she wasn't able to do her job.

'All right, then, let's get both patients into the ambulance.'

He went outside with the ambulance crew, supervising the transfer of the men, and Allison called the hospital and alerted them to be on standby. As she ended the call, she glanced around and saw that a small group of people had gathered, presumably coming out from the surrounding industrial units in order to see what had happened.

'Allison?'

She turned as she recognised that familiar voice, and her heart lifted when she saw his long, lanky figure. 'Nick…it's good to see you.' She drank in his features, her gaze skimming over his sun-bleached hair. 'I was worried when we had the callout in case it was you that was hurt. I'm so glad that it turned out not to be the case.'

'You know me…I'm very careful.' Nick smiled at her. 'Is everything going all right? I know some of the people who work over here, and I'd hate to think that any one of them is badly hurt.'

'We won't know exactly what's wrong until we get them back to the hospital and do scans and tests,' she told him. 'For the moment, they're both doing as well as we can hope for in the circumstances.' She looked back at the ambulance, checking on the progress of the transfer. 'I'll have to go,' she said. 'I need to be in the ambulance with them.'

Nick gave a quick nod. 'I saw that it was you

when the ambulance car arrived, so I rushed into the office to pick this up for you—it's just a toy I've been working on for Connor. I've been meaning to bring it over to you these last couple of weeks, but we've been trying to finish off a special order and it's meant that we've been on the go the whole time.' He handed her a package and she gave him a swift hug.

'Come over and see us as soon as you have some free time,' she said. 'Connor loves being with you.'

'I will.'

Taylor walked over to the ambulance car. 'Nick.' He inclined his head towards her brother in a noncommittal greeting.

'Taylor.' Nick was very still for a moment, and then his mouth compressed before he turned away and walked back into his workshop.

Allison's heart was heavy as she stepped into the ambulance. Would these two men never resolve their differences? Being older than she was, her brother had always looked out for her, but now it looked as though the tables were turning, and it was she who needed to be supportive of him.

The ambulance driver made good speed on the way to the hospital, but by the time they arrived at their destination her patient had slipped into unconsciousness. Hurriedly she secured his airway with an endotracheal tube, making sure that he was receiving a high level of oxygen.

Taylor's patient, Dave, was less of a worry. He was becoming more aware of what was going on around him, and he was asking what had happened, though some of his words were muddled and she guessed the disturbed flow of blood to his brain had caused some damage.

'You passed out for a while,' she told him. 'We don't know why it happened, but we're taking you to the hospital for tests. It may be that your blood vessels have narrowed, causing small clots to form and cause a blockage in the arteries that supply blood to the brain. Or it could be that small cells in your blood have become sticky and are causing problems.'

He frowned, and tried to say something, and she guessed that he wanted to know how they would find out what had gone wrong.

'We'll do blood tests, a chest X-ray and a

tracing of your heart activity. None of that is anything to worry about. Once we have a clearer picture of what we're dealing with, we can start treatment.'

Taylor was on hand as soon as they arrived back at A and E, and he quickly gave instructions to the team about the tests he wanted done. Then he went with Allison to the resuscitation room to supervise James's treatment.

'We'll do a peritoneal lavage,' he said, once they had the scan results. 'The scan doesn't show us what we need to know, but from his symptoms we know there's something bad going on in the abdomen. I'm going to run in 500 ccs of normal saline through a catheter into the abdominal cavity and siphon it out.'

She worked with him on that, and while the procedure was going on, the surgeon came into the room.

He noted the cloudiness of the siphoned liquid and said, 'There must be a tear somewhere. We need to take him up to Theatre so that I can repair it.'

'You did well to pick up on that,' Taylor said,

sometime later as she was writing up her notes. 'It isn't always easy to diagnose abdominal injury.'

'What do you think his chances will be?' Allison was afraid that things might not go too well for their patient. She wanted to stay around and wait for the results, but she was conscious that it was nearing the end of her shift, and she needed to be home for Connor.

'The surgeon is a good man. He knows what he's doing, and we discovered the problem in quick time. The biggest worry for James is that an infection could start up and overwhelm him, but you've started antibiotics, and everything possible is being done to put things right.'

'That's true.' She sent him a fleeting glance. 'Are you going to check up on the other man now? I'd like to come with you to see how he's doing. I don't think he suffered a complete stroke, but I'm interested to know what happened to him.'

'Of course.' He returned her gaze. 'It must have been good for you to see your brother this morning.'

'I think the world of Nick. It's been a struggle

for him to build up the business, but he's never given up on the idea, and I want things to go well for him. He had such great plans. I just wish that he could find a girl to share his dreams, but he always says that living with Mum and Dad made him wary of letting anyone get close.'

Taylor's eyes darkened a fraction. 'I know that he was always very protective of you. He said that you would both hide away, listening to your parents argue, and you would hunch up and flinch at every raised voice.'

Allison nodded. 'We were very young when the marriage broke down, and we were afraid that they would split up and our cosy world would disintegrate. Of course, that's exactly what happened. We spent our teenage years going from one parent to the other, and there was never any security, any feeling of well-being. I suppose that's why Nick and I have always been so close to one another.'

It was also one of the reasons why she, like Nick, was guarded about letting anyone into her life. Nothing was permanent, nothing was guaranteed to be for ever, and she had learned that it was safer to keep away from situations that could draw her into any kind of involvement. It was better for her child, too, because she had learned that children were often hurt when relationships failed.

They walked over to the treatment bay where Dave was resting in bed, propped up against pillows. He looked very much better than he had done earlier, but he was a little agitated.

'I remember that my workmate, James, was coming towards me just before I passed out,' he said, looking at Allison. 'I heard him shout out. Is he all right?'

Allison hesitated before she answered him. She was pleased that he had recovered his speech, although he still stumbled over one or two words, but she was unhappy at what she had to tell him.

'He was pinned back against the storage boxes by the load forks and the body of the truck,' she told him. 'It caused some injury to his abdomen, and he's having surgery at the moment. As soon as I have any news, I'll come and let you know.'

Dave made a low groan and closed his eyes. 'I'm so sorry. I wasn't sure what went on. Everything happened so quickly.'

'It wasn't your fault,' Taylor murmured, glancing up from a folder of papers. 'You were taken ill, and you couldn't prevent what happened. People should know to stand clear when a forklift is in motion.'

'Even so. He's my friend, and he tried to help me.'

'Let's concentrate on your health for the moment,' Taylor said. 'I've been going through your test results, and it looks as though several things have combined to cause your problem. There seem to be a number of factors, such as high blood pressure and high cholesterol, so I think we'll work to change those things, and in the meantime we'll start you on low-dose aspirin. I'm going to get in touch with your general practitioner, and outline the treatment plan that we need to follow.'

Taylor and Allison spoke to Dave for a few minutes longer, and when they had reassured themselves that he was feeling a little calmer, they left him in the care of the nurse.

They walked towards the central desk, and Allison went to collect her bag from a locker nearby. 'I expect that I'll see you on Monday,' she said.

Taylor glanced at the gold watch on his wrist, and she absently noted the light bronze of his skin and the smattering of dark hair that disappeared beneath his cuff. A flash of memory surged through her, of hands that were strong and capable, of his touch that was light as gossamer, his fingers gentle, trailing a fiery path over the softness of her flesh. Heat ricocheted through her, and she closed her eyes briefly, trying to shut out the vision.

'Are you going off duty now?' he said, shooting her a quick look.

She recovered herself. 'Yes, why? Was there something you wanted me to do?'

He shook his head. 'No. It's just that, when we came from the ambulance, I saw you leave a parcel behind the desk, and I thought you might have forgotten that it was there.' He frowned. 'Perhaps you didn't mean to take it home with you.'

'Oh…no, you're right. It had slipped my mind.' She went to retrieve the box, and when she came back towards Taylor, she put it on the desk in front of her and pulled in a deep breath.

She said, 'Nick gave this to me.' Carefully, she removed the lid from the box to reveal a small wooden horse, cleverly designed, with limbs that moved independently of each other. It was beautiful in its simplicity, and she lifted it out and said, 'We were talking about this kind of toy a little while ago, me and Nick. You put the horse on a slope and it walks downhill by itself.'

Taylor ran a finger over the carved wood. 'He's a marvellous craftsman, your brother.' He studied her thoughtfully. 'Is it a piece of nostalgia from your childhood, or did he make it for someone else? I know that Rhea has a little girl. Is it meant for her?'

'No.' She hesitated. 'Actually, he made it for my little boy.' She looked at him directly, her green eyes troubled. 'You see, I have a son. His name's Connor.'

Taylor stared at her. For a long while he said nothing, and then his jaw lifted and he seemed to gather himself together.

'How old is he?'

'He's just four. He started nursery school just a couple of months ago.' In fact, he was a few months over four years old, but she wasn't going to go into details about that. She didn't want him to start working out the relevant dates.

His gaze ran over her, as though he was seeing her for the first time. 'I ought to have realised that things wouldn't stand still. I always knew that you had a thing going with Nick's partner.' His mouth straightened. 'I suppose he must be the father. You and Ben were always together, and I wondered if that's why you were so interested in having a part in the business, albeit just a monetary one.'

He glanced at her left hand. 'I see that you're not wearing a ring. Does that mean that you're not together any more?'

'We're just friends,' she said, and Taylor frowned.

'Does he live with you?'

'No.' She wasn't sure what to make of his assumption that Ben was the father. That one time that she and Taylor had come together, he had tried to ensure that she would not become pregnant, and they had both relied on the fact that she had been taking a contraceptive pill to regulate her body's hormones. Perhaps now he believed that she had been taking it because of a relationship with Ben.

At the time, it hadn't occurred to her that the Pill might fail to protect her, but she had been ill for a brief time previously and had taken antibiotics. Taylor didn't know that, and maybe that made it impossible for him to imagine that the child might be his.

Ought to she to tell him the truth? So far, Connor hadn't asked any questions about his daddy, but he needed a father, she was very much aware of that, and as he grew up, he would feel the loss more and more.

But hadn't Greg said that very morning that Taylor wouldn't be staying around for long? What effect would that have on Connor, to get to know his father and then to lose him again?

Maybe it was enough for the moment that Taylor managed to come to terms with the fact that she had a child. She would try to deal with the rest of her problems later.

CHAPTER FOUR

TAYLOR was busy treating a patient for a suspected brain haemorrhage when Allison went into work on Monday morning, but he glanced at her as she passed by the resuscitation bay and inclined his head in a brief greeting. His mouth made a grim line, and that could have been because he was concerned for his patient, but Allison wasn't sure about that.

She didn't get to talk to him from then onwards, even though she saw him from time to time, dealing with a steady stream of patients, and she began to wonder whether he was making a deliberate effort to stay away from her. Was he still brooding over the fact that she had a child? He had seemed to be shaken by her news, and she wasn't sure quite why it would have affected him that way.

Perhaps he had misgivings about Ben and was doubtful about his role in her life. He had always rubbed along reasonably well with Nick and his colleague, but had something happened to change his opinion about them, or about the way they were running the business, and after a disagreement with both of the men, he had started to distance himself from them.

Or was his reaction to her simply governed by the fact that he felt it was wrong for her to bring up a child on her own without the father being around? In that case, it was all the more confusing that it hadn't occurred to him that Connor might be his son.

'Will you take a look at a patient for me?' Sarah asked, putting her head around the door of the side room where Allison was doing some simple lab tests. 'He's a young man, around sixteen years old, and I think he's been taking drugs of some sort. I've put him on a heart monitor and I'm giving him oxygen. He's not making much sense, and he's very agitated. He's grinding his teeth and clenching his jaw quite a lot and complaining of blurred vision.'

Sarah gave a slight shudder and winced. 'His name's Harry. His friends conveniently disappeared after they dropped him off here, but before he ran off, one of them gave some information about his family and said he'd taken ecstasy. They'd all been hanging around together in the City. Apparently there's a protest march about something or other supposed to be going off somewhere near Parliament Square this afternoon, and it looks as though a few people are getting into a party spirit ahead of time.' She frowned. 'I thought marches were banned around there, so I'm sure there'll be trouble.'

'You're probably right.' Allison went to take a look at the boy. She was thankful to be able to immerse herself in her work. It was far better for her to do that than to dwell on what might be going on in Taylor's head.

'Some party,' she murmured, shaking her head in sad disbelief when she saw the teenager. 'He looks as though he's barely more than a child, and he's all skin and bones.' She glanced at Sarah. 'Do we have an address or a phone number for his family?'

'According to the friend, he lives with his mother. He gave me a contact number, and I've been trying to get in touch with her, but she's not answering her phone.'

The boy was becoming feverish and was very agitated. His heart was racing and his body was showing signs of tremor.

'Harry, I'm Dr Matthews,' Allison said gently, 'and I'm going to look after you. I'm going to put something into your arm so that we can give you medication through a tube. It should help to make you feel a little better.'

Harry moved restlessly, waving his arms about in a wild fashion, and Allison grimaced.

'I'm not going to be able to get a needle in anywhere unless someone can come and help us to hold him still for a while.'

'I'll help out with that,' Taylor said, coming into the treatment room, and Allison glanced up at him, taken unawares by his sudden appearance.

'Thanks. I didn't realise you were free just yet.' She tried to collect her thoughts, disturbed by this sudden vision of him looking fresh and energetic in beautifully fitted dark trousers and a pale linen shirt.

'We need to do a full range of tests,' she told Sarah in a quiet tone, 'but we'll start him on supportive therapy straight away, because he looks as though he's going downhill fast. Unfortunately, there's no specific antidote to ecstasy. We'll get some activated charcoal inside him as soon as possible and I'll give him an injection of diazepam to control the agitation. I'm also worried about the cardiac arrhythmia, and the hypertension, because there's always a danger of an intracerebral haemorrhage, so I'll treat that with a beta blocker and hope that it calms things down. If we don't act quickly, he could go into full cardiac arrest.'

'You might still have to intubate him to protect the airway.' Taylor's expression reflected her own bleak thoughts.

'Yes.'

'What about seizures?' Sarah wanted to know. 'He's been showing signs of pre-convulsive movements. Will the diazepam be sufficient to prevent those?'

Allison nodded. 'I'm hoping so. It may be necessary to set up an infusion if his condition worsens. Whatever happens, you'll need to monitor him very closely, and let me know if there's any change.'

'I will.'

Some time later, she moved out of the treatment room and into the general area of A and E. Taylor went with her, stopping by the desk to pick up another chart.

'You're worried about him, aren't you?' he said, flicking her sideways glance.

'I am.' She jotted down a few notes in the boy's file, adding softly, 'It's heartbreaking to see anyone who is ruining their life through drug taking, but when it's a teenager who gets caught up in it, things seem even worse. If we manage to get him over this episode, I suppose all we can do is refer him for rehabilitation.'

He nodded. 'We'll do what we can for him. I've had a quick look at his file, and perhaps we can put the family in touch with a counsellor. The father isn't around, is he?'

'Apparently not, according to his friend, but

he has a mother and a couple of sisters, by all accounts.'

Taylor's mouth made a straight line. 'Perhaps not having a father figure is part of the problem. Either way, drug taking isn't just an issue for the user. It affects everyone who cares about him.'

'The lack of a father isn't necessarily a reason for children going off the rails. My own father wasn't around very much when Nick and I were teenagers, but neither of us went off track. Besides, it's probably better to have an absent father rather than one who is a bully or a tyrant.'

'That's one way of looking at it.' He gave her a thoughtful glance. 'So you're not too concerned about your own child not being part of a two-parent family?'

'I didn't say that. I just meant to say that these things happen, and it doesn't have to be a full-blown disaster. Many women bring up their children successfully without having a man around.'

'Hmm. Maybe they do.' He glanced through the chart. 'I imagine your little boy is at school today? No matter what you say, it must be difficult for you, finding a balance between work and home life.'

'The truth is, Connor will always come first.' She glanced at him, wondering if the boss part of him would dispute that. He didn't make any comment, though, and she carefully replaced the file in the tray. 'Actually, the school is closed for the day. The teachers are there, but they're having one of their special consultation days, where they deal with administration and so on.'

He frowned. 'So who is looking after him? I expect you must have arrangements in place for all kinds of situations that might crop up like that.'

'I do. It's mostly Rhea who looks after him. She doesn't live too far away from me, though a neighbour helps out occasionally. I drop him off at Rhea's house and she takes him to school if I'm on early shift, and she takes care of him at the end of the school day. Connor and her little girl usually get on well together, and they're company for one another.'

'That must work out well for you. It must be

fun for your boy to have someone around his own age to play with.'

'It is, and they get to go on outings together. Like today, Rhea said she would take them to St James's Park this morning—after she had been to Covent Garden to deliver some costumes to one of the theatre companies there. She has a contract with them and lately she's been working on some specialist alterations that they needed urgently. I just hope they don't get caught up in this protest march that I keep hearing about.'

Her brows drew together in a fine line. 'She sometimes calls in to see me at the hospital if she's in the area, especially if she has the children with her, so it's possible that she might stop by today. Apparently Connor is always asking if he can see his mum at work.' She sent him a quick glance. 'I hope that's all right with you. Obviously, I wouldn't let it interfere with my work.'

'That's OK. As to the march, I wouldn't worry too much about it, if I were you. Rhea's always had a good head on her shoulders. She'll know how to keep out of the way, and St James's Park is tranquil enough. I expect they'll be feeding the geese and the pelicans around the lake, not to mention the ducks.'

He gave her a quizzical look. 'It's hard for me to imagine you with a little boy.' He was thoughtful for a moment or two, and then he said, 'My sister's children are always agitating to go out and about, and I imagine Connor is the same. Working full time must cause a few problems for you in that respect.'

'I take him out whenever I can…but you're right, it isn't always easy.'

'Does his father help you out with any of it?'

His question startled her and took the wind out of her sails. 'I… No, actually, he doesn't.' It was a truthful enough answer, but he was frowning and she swallowed hard and hoped he would leave it at that for now. She simply wasn't ready to fill him in on the whole story just yet. 'Anyway, it doesn't matter,' she said. 'My brother is always ready to lend a hand. He loves Connor to bits and he often spends time with him, doing boy things, like making paper aeroplanes or flying kites and so on.'

'I suppose you must get to see a lot more of him now that he's moved back into the City.'

'Yes, I do. In fact, I said that I would meet him later on today for a pizza at a place not too far from the hospital. He and Ben are in town this afternoon, looking for materials for a special project they're working on. I planned on taking my lunch-break later than usual, so that it would fit in with their timetable.'

Taylor's expression was brooding. 'Ben must be glad that they were able to turn the business around after the way their first efforts dive-bombed.'

'Yes, I'm sure he is.' She was wary of saying much to him where Ben was concerned, given his reaction when she had told him that she had a child. Ben had always been her friend, and it was true that they had dated at one time, but Taylor's view of him had always been somewhat reserved. His manner towards him might be even more strained now, and a feeling of guilt washed over her. She was doing Ben an injustice by letting Taylor go on thinking that he was Connor's father.

Taylor looked as though he might have said something more, but at that moment paramedics brought a man into A and E, and Taylor hurried away to examine him.

Allison went to look in on her drug user patient once more, and tried not to think about the part Taylor might have played in her brother's downfall, or about Connor's lack of a father.

Sarah must have managed to get in touch with Harry's mother, because she finally arrived at the hospital some twenty minutes later in an agitated state.

'What's happened to him? They said he had collapsed.' Her breath was coming in short bursts. 'Is he going to be all right?' She was shaking, her nerves in shreds.

'Perhaps you would like to come with me into the relatives' room,' Allison suggested. 'We can be quiet in there, and I'll be able to talk to you about his condition and tell you what we're doing for him.'

'Will I be able to see him?'

'Yes, of course. I've just put a tube down his throat to help with his breathing, so I don't want you to be alarmed by that when you go to him. It's part of our normal procedure. The nurse is with him at the moment, trying to bring down his temperature. As soon as she's finished, I'll take you to him.'

It was some time before Allison was able to go back to the central desk and catch up on her case notes, but no sooner had she started to write up the first file than Rhea walked into the unit with Poppy and Connor in tow.

'Hi, Rhea.' Allison greeted her friend, before holding out her arms to Connor and giving him a kiss. Then she turned to Poppy and gave the little girl a hug. 'Have you had a good time?' she asked, looking from one to the other.

Poppy nodded, looking pleased. 'Yes, we did. We went on the swings.'

'And then we had sandwiches and pop,' Connor said, 'and we listened to the band playing music, and we went on the bridge over the water and we seed the London Eye.' He paused for breath and looked directly at Allison. 'I want to go on the London Eye, and I want to see the palace where the Queen lives. Can we, Mummy?'

'One day, perhaps,' Allison said. 'We might go in the summer, when I have some time off work.'

Connor frowned, unsure as to whether or not he liked that answer, and he opened his mouth to say something, but closed it again as he caught sight of Taylor walking towards them. He stared up at him, studying his features with curiosity.

Allison held her breath, haunted by the knowledge that father and son were coming face to face for the first time. Would Taylor recognise the similarities between the two of them? Would he guess that this was his child? Her heart was in her mouth as she watched them.

'Who are you?' Connor asked, his wide eyes a solemn reflection of his father's grey gaze.

Taylor smiled and brought himself down to Connor's height, bending his knees in one fluid, easy motion. 'I'm Taylor,' he said. 'Dr Briscoe. I work here with your mother.'

Connor was frowning again. 'I know 'bout you. Mummy told me you said she was all dusty, but it wasn't her fault. It was 'cos she'd been in a hole in a building what fell down.'

'Ah...yes, I did say that, didn't I?' A look of

bemusement crossed Taylor's face, and Allison groaned inwardly. Connor's memory was as sharp as a needle, and she ought to have known that he would bring up something like that.

Taylor tried to make amends. 'I'm sorry about that,' he murmured in a tentative fashion, studying Connor's expression. 'I really didn't mean it in a bad way.'

'That's all right,' Connor said, airily dismissive. 'I said she was dusty, as well, 'cos she tells me off when I get mud on my clothes. She says I'm a urchin.'

Taylor tried in vain to suppress a grin. 'That's what mothers do, don't they? They sometimes tell you things you don't want to hear. But you got your own back. You told her, didn't you?'

Connor nodded, clearly captivated by his new confidant, and he watched with interest as Taylor turned his attention to Poppy.

Allison dragged her gaze away from father and son and glanced at Rhea. Her friend looked harassed, and when Allison looked at her more closely, she suspected that she was troubled, too.

'Is something wrong?' she asked. 'Have the children been hassling you?'

'No, it's nothing like that,' Rhea said in a low voice, glancing at the children as they chatted with Taylor. 'They've been just perfect today...taking in everything and running about, getting rid of their energy on the grass in the park.'

'But something's bothering you, isn't it? I recognise that haunted look from way back. I remember how you were when Steve was causing problems for you.' Allison looked at Rhea searchingly and saw that she had hit a nerve. 'Is that it? Is he following you again? I thought you had finally managed to give him the slip last year.'

Rhea's face had paled. 'So did I, but I think he's back again.' She grimaced. 'I was going to take the children to my place because we were running late, but just as I turned the car into the street, I thought I saw him walking towards my house. Everything about him looked familiar... the way his hair fell below his ears in waves, his stocky build. He stopped at my door and seemed to be looking in at the windows.'

'Do you think there's any chance that you could be mistaken?'

'I don't think so. I caught a glimpse of his face as I drove past him. There was no way I was going to stop the car with him stalking the neighbourhood.' Her mouth made an odd shape. 'Anyway, there have been other things…things that didn't quite add up at the time. Someone tried to break into the house, but the man who lives next door came to see what was going on and he must have scared him away. Then, another day, a man rang the theatre, asking for me. He wouldn't leave a name.'

Allison felt a tugging at her skirt. She looked down to see that Connor was waiting to be heard, and immediately she began to worry about how long he had been listening in.

'I seed the man,' he said. 'I 'membered him from before, a long time ago. His name's Steve. I don't like him.'

Allison's lungs contracted. 'When was this?'

He shrugged. 'Dunno. It was the other day. We was playing in the garden at Poppy's house and he was coming down the street.'

'What did you do? Did you speak to him?'

'No. I don't like him 'cos he shouts, so I telled Poppy to come in the house and play. She didn't want to, so I chased her.'

Allison hugged him close and ruffled his hair, and when she looked up, she saw that Taylor was watching her. He must have picked up on her alarm at the situation, because he moved towards her and said softly, 'The boy did the right thing, and it's good that no harm came to either of them.'

He looked down at Connor. 'There's a box of toys in the corner of the waiting room over there, and there's a table full of construction bricks, so you could make a truck or a house. Would you and Poppy like to go and play with them for a while?'

Connor nodded eagerly, and both children slid their hands into his and let him lead them to the play area.

When Taylor came back a moment later, he said, 'I think it's fairly obvious that Rhea guessed right, and Steve is back in the area.'

He sent Rhea a quick look. 'It must be

worrying for you,' he said, his brows drawing together. 'Have you thought about what you're going to do? Will you talk to the police about it?'

'I suppose I'll have to.' Rhea's face took on an anguished look. 'I don't feel safe going back home. He's been violent in the past, and I don't want to go through all that again.' She seemed to be thinking aloud. 'I suppose I could go and stay at my parents' house for a while, but they live some distance away and I need to be close at hand for my work…and there's Poppy's school, of course.'

Allison collected her thoughts. 'Do you want to come and stay at my place for a while? He won't be able to find you there, will he?'

'Would you mind if I did that?' Rhea looked relieved. 'It would give me a bit of breathing space.'

'Of course I don't mind. It'll be a bit cramped, but we'll make the best of it.'

'Thank you.' Rhea put a hand to her chest as though she was nursing a pain deep down. 'I don't think I'd sleep easily in my own house, knowing that he's around.'

Allison went and found her bag from behind the central desk and brought out her front-door key. 'Take this,' she said, 'and go and make yourself at home.'

'Thanks,' Rhea said. 'You're an angel. I really hate to burden you like this.'

'It isn't a problem.' Allison glanced down at the watch on her wrist. 'I'm going for my lunch-break in a while, so why don't we go together? I said I would meet up with Nick and Ben for a coffee and something to eat. Perhaps one of them would go back with you to your house, and then, if the coast's clear, you can pick up a few things.'

Rhea thought about it. 'That's a good idea. I think I might do that, if one of the men will come with me.' She hesitated, and her face crumpled momentarily. 'I'm going to have to find myself a new place, aren't I? I had hoped that I'd finished moving around, but if he's in the area, I don't see how I can live in that house any more. I daren't risk it.'

Taylor had been quiet for a while, but now he said, 'Are you sure about that? How long do you plan to keep on running? Perhaps it's time to settle this problem once and for all.'

Rhea shook her head. 'I don't know how I can do that. I wish it didn't always have to come to this, and I hate to have to move Poppy all over again, just as we were getting settled, but I can't think of any alternative. She worries if she thinks Steve is anywhere near. I don't want her to be upset, and I don't want to spend my life living in fear.'

'I realise this must be really difficult for you.' Taylor threw her a sympathetic glance.

Allison could see that he was thinking things through. 'You know, Rhea,' he said at last, 'you should think about it some more, and not make any snap decisions, but if, after a while, you're still determined to move away, I might be able to help you. I inherited some properties from my grandparents, and mostly they've been rented out to tenants, but I could have a word with the agent to see if we've anything that would suit you.'

'Would you?' Rhea's eyes brightened. 'Oh, that's brilliant, thanks. That would be such a weight off my mind.'

Taylor gave her an encouraging smile. 'It might be possible to find you a secure place that's close to the local police station…and in the meantime, you could apply for an injunction to keep him from harassing you. The police might set you up with an alarm call system so that they could get to you quickly in case of trouble. If things work out, you might not need to move.' He paused to gauge her reaction to that, and when she gave a slight nod, he said, 'Leave it with me, then, and I'll make a few enquiries so that you'll know what your options are. You don't have to make up your mind about anything right now. Go and enjoy lunch with Allison and the children, and try to stay calm.'

'Thanks. I'm beginning to feel a bit better already.' Rhea attempted a smile. 'I haven't been able to think straight since I saw him. My first reaction was to come here.'

'That's understandable,' Allison murmured. 'I'm glad you came to us.'

Rhea looked over to the waiting room. 'I'd better go and see to the children,' she said.

She moved away from them and Allison

glanced at Taylor. It was heart-warming that he was so ready to step in and try to help but, then, she had always known that he was a compassionate, caring man. It was one of the qualities that had endeared him to her years ago.

Perhaps it had also been her downfall, because when he had come to her aid on that snowy night so long ago, she had gone into his arms without a second thought, driven only by a need to be close to him, wanting to submerge herself in the kisses he gave so passionately.

He glanced at her now and she hoped that the warm colour that must show in her cheeks would not give her thoughts away. 'It was good of you to offer to do that for Rhea,' she murmured. 'Do you really think you'll be able to find her somewhere safe to stay?'

'I'll do my best. My grandparents bought properties in good areas. They had an eye for safety issues, so I expect we'll be able to come up with something suitable. She really needs to deal with the situation, though, and get him off her back once and for all. That means involving the police.'

He frowned, giving her a long look. 'Besides,

she has two young children in her care, and it's important that they should be safe. You must be worried for your son, knowing that Steve might come around.'

'I am.' Allison pressed her lips together. 'I hadn't realised that Connor had seen him hanging around Rhea's place, but that explains a lot about his behaviour. At school, they said he's been distracted lately, and not his usual self, and now I think I have a good idea as to what was behind all that.'

Taylor put an arm around her and lightly squeezed her shoulder. 'It can't be easy for you. I know my sister worries about what goes on in the children's heads sometimes, and I'm glad I don't have to deal with those kinds of problems. I have enough concerns already, trying to get to grips with issues at work.'

Allison's nerve endings jumped in response to his touch. His nearness sent her defences into overdrive, and for a moment or two she didn't know how to counteract the dizzying effect of his gentle caress.

Then common sense took over and she made

an effort to bolster her resources. It didn't mean anything to him. It was just a casual embrace, a closeness that was meant to cheer her up and let her know that she wasn't alone.

'I'll get by,' she said, and he let his arm drop to his side. She knew then that she had been right all along not to tell him about Connor. Why was she trying to delude herself? He didn't want a child in his life. Neither did he want any meaningful relationship with her. Work was his mistress. It fuelled his ambitions and she was a poor second, left waiting somewhere in the wings.

CHAPTER FIVE

'WOULD you come and take a look at Mrs Francis for me?' Sarah asked, coming over to the desk and glancing at Taylor. 'She fell down the stairs and injured her spine, but she's back from X-Ray now. I would say that she's all right, but I'd like a second opinion.'

'OK, I'll be right with you.' Taylor headed towards the examination room with the nurse, leaving Allison to tie up any loose ends before she went out to lunch with Rhea and the children. She handed over the care of her patients to the registrar, leaving note of her whereabouts with the desk clerk who was on duty.

'I'm on call, so I might have to leave you all at short notice,' she told Rhea, 'but Nick and Ben will be there with you if that happens.'

'Do you think you'll get called out?' Rhea asked.

'It doesn't happen that often. It's mostly when something major happens in the City, or there's an event going on and trouble breaks out.' She made a face. 'Like the march that's going on today, but with any luck nothing untoward will happen. That's the reason why I don't want to stray too far from the hospital, though.' She smiled. 'It's lucky that we all like pizza.'

She was glad to be with Rhea and the children. Any moments that she managed to spend with her son were precious to her, like gold dust.

Nick and Ben were already waiting at the restaurant, seated at a table by the window that looked out onto the street, and soon everyone was gathered around, eating their fill. Allison chose a pizza that was spread with a thick tomato paste and topped with cheese, sweet corn and peppers, and Connor had his favourite.

'I like the pieces of ham in it,' he said, his eyes widening, 'and the mushroom. It tastes yummy.'

The children had ice-cream milkshakes to wash the food down, and were soon showing off strawberry moustaches where the froth had settled around their mouths.

Rhea told the men about her temporary move to Allison's house. 'I'm not sure how long I'll be staying there,' she said, looking anxious. 'Taylor said he would try to find me a place if I should decide to leave my own home for good, but I've no idea how long that will take.'

'I'm sure he'll find you something,' Nick murmured. 'He wouldn't have said it if he didn't have something in mind.'

'He's always had an interest in being a landlord,' Ben added. He was about the same age as Nick, in his early thirties, and he had crisp black hair and grey-blue eyes that were open and honest. 'Everyone expected him to sell the properties that he inherited, thinking that they would be too much trouble for him, but he kept them on. That's how we came to rent the premises for our business when we first started up. It was local and we had a lot of contacts in the area, and we thought everything would be plain sailing.'

Nick made a face. 'Until he gave us notice to

quit.' He glanced at Rhea. 'I'm sure he won't do the same with you,' he added hastily. 'He told us he wanted to sell the unit and only keep residential properties on the books. Something to do with the rating system, he said, but I think it was just an excuse. For some reason, he backed off from having anything to do with the business, and he seemed to want us out of there. He refused to renew our lease, and things went downhill for us from then on.'

'It wasn't just a problem with the premises that caused the slide, though,' Ben said, stopping to lick tomato from his fingers. 'We had a problem with identity theft and we lost some of our clients because of it. They bought goods from us by credit card and then found that money was being taken from their accounts without their knowledge. They assumed this happened through their dealings with us, but we had no idea it was going on until it was too late, and it made life very difficult for us. Our reputation as a company was shattered.'

He frowned. 'Taylor never mentioned that he knew anything about it, but perhaps he came to hear of it somehow. That might have had some bearing on his decision.'

'Surely he would have given you the benefit of the doubt?' Rhea said. 'I can't imagine that he would throw you out of your premises without looking into things first.'

'I guess we'll never know. He didn't ever talk to us about how we operated the business. I thought it was because he was our landlord and didn't want to pry.' Ben's expression was resigned, but then he straightened up and said in a firm tone, 'Anyway, Rhea, if you want me to come and fit special locks or safety chains in your house, or devise some system to protect you, just let me know. Whatever you decide to do, we're all here to help.'

'Thanks, Ben. I appreciate that.'

Allison's bleeper went off just then and she grimaced, swallowing the last of her coffee before pausing to check the text message. 'I'll have to go,' she said. 'There's been some trouble near Westminster, and there are a number of casualties. Taylor's on his way to pick me up.'

She explained to Connor what was happening and then gathered up her bag and jacket, preparing to leave. 'I'll be home in a little while,' she told Connor, giving him a kiss. 'Be good, won't you?'

'I will. Can Uncle Nick come home wiv us? I want to show him how my horse goes down the slope.'

'I don't know, sweetheart. He might have to work.' She sent her brother a quick look.

'I'll see if I can come over to you later on, Connor. Maybe this evening.'

Connor appeared to be satisfied with that answer for the moment. He waved his drinking straw over Poppy's milkshake. 'You've got some left,' he said.

'So have you.' Poppy retaliated, pulling her glass out of his reach.

'It looks as though Taylor's here already,' Ben said, glancing out of the window a minute or so later. 'He must have paged you as he was setting out.'

'He probably did. We don't have much time to hang about when we're on call.'

Ben saw her to the door of the restaurant and gave her a hug. 'I'll give Rhea a hand collecting her stuff from the house,' he said. 'Don't worry.'

'Thanks. That will make me feel easier in my mind.'

She hurried out to the waiting car and slid into the passenger seat, giving him a wave as Taylor accelerated away.

'I see that you two are still very close,' he murmured, keeping his eyes on the road ahead. His mouth jutted a little, as though he was deep in thought.

'I… Yes. We are.' She sent him an oblique glance. 'I don't think I ever said that we weren't. In fact…' She hesitated, thinking things through. 'Perhaps you might have assumed too much. Like you said, Ben and I have always been good friends.'

His eyes narrowed on her. 'You're right, I might have picked up on the wrong idea. A lot has happened in the last few years, and maybe things have changed for both of us.'

There was a bleak edge to his tone that she couldn't quite fathom, but by now they had reached their destination, and there wasn't any more time left to question him about it.

A large crowd had assembled in the square, and police were keeping them back by use of a manned cordon. Taylor parked the car next to the ambulance that was already in attendance, and opened the boot to bring out the medical equipment.

'You brought my bag,' Allison said. 'That was good thinking. I wondered if we might have to share.'

She sent a glance over her immediate surroundings and saw that several people were being treated for a variety of injuries. One man looked as though he had a fractured arm and another had a broken nose. There was at least one other doctor tending to the casualties and she guessed he had come along with the ambulance crew.

A police officer escorted them to their patients. 'We've had all sorts of trouble,' he said. 'People surging forward and causing crush injuries, and a bad element in the crowd looking to cause trouble. Judging from some of the casualties a few of them from rent-a-mob must have been carrying concealed weapons.'

He directed Taylor to where a man was suffering from what appeared to be heart-attack symptoms, and then he led Allison to someone who was lying on the ground.

'There was a fight,' he said, 'but when we tried to intervene to break it up a man escaped into the crowd, and we found this fellow lying on the pavement. It looks like an opportunist mugging. There's always someone who will try his luck. We think the man's wallet and mobile phone were stolen, and he's been stabbed. The paramedics have been taking care of him, but it looks pretty bad to me.'

Allison knelt down to examine the man. He was around thirty years old, she guessed, and he was groaning with pain. That didn't surprise her. He had obviously tried to put up a fight and he had been kicked and punched for his trouble. There was a stab wound to his chest, causing him to lose a lot of blood.

'His breathing's shallow, respirations 38, and the heart rate is 138,' the paramedic said.

'Breath sounds are decreased on the left side. The pulse oximetry meter shows very low oxygen saturation. Whoever did this meant business. He wasn't intending for him to get up and run after him.'

'You're right,' Allison agreed. 'He's not doing too well at all.' She frowned as she examined the man and tried to locate the stab wound. 'The vein in his neck is distended, which makes me wonder if the knife penetrated the diaphragm. A tear in that position would allow the abdominal organs to move up into the chest cavity and displace the lung.'

'What are you going to do?' the paramedic asked.

'I'll put in a nasogastric tube. That should help to decompress the stomach. We'll give him saline and add a second line with lactated Ringer's solution.'

'Shall I give him pain relief?'

'Yes, please, do.'

By the time they had finished working with him, the patient was becoming a little more responsive and Allison said, 'Has the pain eased at all?'

The man nodded, but speaking was too much of an effort for him.

'We'll get you back to the hospital and do a CT scan, and then you'll need to have surgery to repair the damage,' Allison told him. He looked as though he had absorbed that information, but it wasn't too long before he started to slip back into unconsciousness. 'Try to stay with us,' Allison said, an urgent note in her voice.

Taylor came to join them. 'How are you doing?' he asked her. 'Do you need any help?'

'Yes, thanks. We need to get him into the ambulance as quickly as possible. I'm going to call ahead to arrange for the surgeon to receive him.'

The paramedics took care of the man until the doctor from their own team came and joined them inside the ambulance. Then the doors closed behind them and as she watched the vehicle move away she could only hope that they had managed to gain their patient a little time.

'Do you think he'll make it?' Taylor asked, sending her an oblique glance.

'I don't know. It depends what other damage was done.' She sighed heavily, and looked around. 'This is all so senseless…a man's life for a wallet and a mobile phone.' She felt sick inside.

'Come on, I'll take you home,' Taylor said, placing a hand in the small of her back and urging her towards the car. 'We've done all that we can here, and your shift was over a while ago.'

'Was it?' She had lost all track of time. She said, 'I should be able to get the tube from here. There's no reason for you to look after me. You'll be needed at the hospital, won't you?'

He shook his head. 'No. I've finished for the day, too. Besides, you're looking pale and a bit shocked, and I feel that I need to watch over you for a while. This has upset you, hasn't it?'

'It has, but I'm not sure why. I've seen all sorts of cases in my time in A and E, but usually there's some sort of explanation for why it happened, some way that perhaps the hurt could have been avoided.'

She waited while he stowed their medical equipment in the boot of the car. 'You feel that sometimes you can show people how to take more care,' she said, 'but there's no solution for this kind of thing. It's pure wickedness, the selfish act on the part of a stranger who cares nothing for anyone else, who simply takes what he wants and isn't bothered how he gets it. How do you fight something like that? How do you stop it from happening?'

Taylor's mouth compressed. 'The short answer is, you can't. We can't put the world to rights because we can't legislate against mankind. All we can do is to try to take care of our own. We can be thankful for the people we do manage to help. It's good when things turn out well, as they did for the man from the tile warehouse.'

'You mean James, the man with the abdominal injury?'

He nodded. 'That's right. I was concerned for him for a time, but he came through surgery all right.'

She frowned. 'The last time I checked up on him, he was feverish, and the nurses were worried about the possibility of septicaemia.'

'I know, but the antibiotics were changed and he's come through it all right.'

'That's good news.'

'Yes, it is.'

The revelation that James was on the mend didn't do anything to lessen her feelings of sadness and disillusion about what had happened today. 'What was this protest march all about, anyway?' she asked. 'Do we know?'

He shrugged. 'There's always a protest about something or other, wars in far-off countries, defence measures—too much, or not enough—council tax, pensions. You name it, someone will take umbrage about it.'

She managed a wry smile, but her overall feeling was still one of dejection.

Taylor moved closer and put an arm around her, and instantly she felt warm and comforted. 'My place is not far from here,' he said quietly. 'Shall we stop by there and get a cup of coffee? Then I'll take you home.'

'Yes, OK. I'd like that.' For some reason she didn't feel that she was ready to go straight home. The events of the day were taking their toll of her.

'Good.' Taylor seemed to be pleased by her response. 'I think you need some space before you go and deal with Rhea and her problems on top of this, and I'm sure you don't want Connor to see you looking distressed. I think your boy's a very astute little chap, and he'll pick up on any downbeat mood straight away. I expect that's why he overheard and told you about seeing Steve. He doesn't miss much, does he?'

'No, he doesn't.' He was like his father in that, she reflected with a wry inward wince. It hadn't taken Taylor long to work out what made Connor tick, had it, or for him to pick up on her mood?

He held open the passenger door for her and she slid into the seat. He was right about her needing some time to get herself together. Besides, she realised that she liked this feeling of being close to him and all her instincts were telling her to prolong it while she could.

She was also curious to discover where he lived. 'Whereabouts is your place?' she asked. 'I imagine it must be fairly close to the hospital.'

He turned his key in the ignition and moved the car out onto the main road. 'I have an apartment in Mayfair. It isn't very big, and there's no garden, but there's a parking facility close by, which is useful. I'm in the triangle between Green Park and Hyde Park, so I feel quite content there. It isn't too far from the hospital by tube, and if I'm feeling energetic and I've time to spare, I can even walk to work some days.'

'It sounds ideal.' She glanced at him, studying him surreptitiously from under her lashes. 'Do you ever go back to the house in Buckinghamshire?'

'As often as I can, though I think Claire visits more frequently than I do. Our parents still live there, and they look forward to seeing the boys. When we're all over there, we try to get out and about, and enjoy the countryside, especially if the weather's fine.'

'I remember that you liked to do that when Nick and I lived in the area, when we were all youngsters. I used to enjoy walking by the river, and just breathing in the fresh air.'

'And we would all go to the beech woods every summer.' There was a far-away look in his eyes. 'We made dens and imagined that we were hiding away from the world in our own secret place.'

She nodded. 'It was fun, wasn't it? We

climbed onto the fallen trees and tried to keep our balance, and then we'd run off and get wet in the brook, and have to dry out before we went home.' She smiled, calling it to mind, and when Taylor parked the car in a garage that was tucked away near his apartment, she saw that he was smiling, too.

It had been a long while ago, but they had been precious days, those times that they'd spent together walking across fields and climbing the stiles, sitting on the fences and laughing with the sheer exuberance of simply being alive and young.

Of course, for Allison, there had always been the added joy of being with Taylor. She had looked up to him, seeing him tall and strong, a leader, full of ideas as to what they should do next. But it had had to end at some point, and eventually they had all gone their separate ways.

'It's just a short walk from here to where I live,' he said now as they stepped out of the car, and he came and placed a hand lightly at her elbow, turning her slightly and showing her the way. It was just a small contact, but even so her whole body warmed in response.

She saw that by now they were in a peaceful residential area that was free of traffic. Together, they walked along a terraced street that was made up of grand Georgian houses. They were mostly stone fronted, with one or two built of red brick, all with iron balconies and projecting porches. They were beautiful in their simplicity.

'One of these is yours?' she asked.

He nodded. 'I have the ground floor and lower floor of my building, which is convenient for me, and it also means that I have a balcony to myself on the upper floor. It isn't very big, but it's good to go out there and take the air in the summer months. There are two floors above my property, which are occupied by another tenant.' He made a wry smile. 'He's lucky, because he gets to have a roof terrace.'

He stopped at an arched doorway that was sheltered by a covered porch, decorated with hanging baskets that bloomed with spring flowers, and Allison looked around. An iron railing fronted the building, and behind it there were flowering shrubs that added a bright splash of colour to the Georgian facade. Taylor put his key in the door lock and ushered her inside.

'It's a communal entrance lobby,' he told her, 'but it's only used by me and my neighbour upstairs. We both work peculiar hours, so sometimes we're ships that pass in the night, so to speak.'

Allison was lost for words as he showed her around the apartment. 'It's perhaps an odd arrangement,' he said, 'but the living room is upstairs.'

The lower ground floor, she discovered, housed two bedrooms, whose windows opened out to the front of the building. Voile curtains lent privacy during the daylight hours, and there were heavier damask drapes that went almost from floor to ceiling and added a touch of opulence.

The rooms were luxuriously fitted out, each with its own *en suite* bathroom, exquisitely designed with frosted glass washbasins and spectacular shower cubicles designed with an eye for superior quality. Next to the stairwell was a small dressing room. She blinked, taking it all in.

'Good heavens. The dressing room is bigger

than my bedroom back home,' she said. 'I'm very impressed.'

He laughed, and she looked at him in wonder, because the smile lit up his face and his grey eyes took on a hint of blue, glittering like sunlight on the ripples of the sea.

'I'm glad you like it,' he said. 'Come and see the other rooms upstairs.'

She hesitated in the hallway, still gazing around at the rooms that led off in either direction, so that Taylor caught hold of her hand in his firm grip and started to draw her away towards the stairs. 'You can always come back and explore them later, if you want.'

His words made her stop and wonder what he meant by that. Picking up on her indecision, he stood for a moment and gave her a look of pure mischief, his head tilted to one side. 'I'd be happy to help you to do that if you wanted to try them for size, but I'd have to recommend the master bedroom. It's by far the most comfortable.'

'Oh,' she said, instantly flustered. 'I was just…'

'I know,' he murmured, his lips making a crooked line. 'I know what you were thinking, but I can always dream, can't I?' He gazed at her, and there was something in his expression that made her limbs begin to melt. He seemed to move closer to her, so that his head was bent towards her and his mouth was just a heartbeat away from hers, but it might only have been her imagination. She was so very much aware of him just then.

He said softly, 'It may have been five years since we were together in any meaningful way, but my memory of it is as clear as ever.'

'Oh,' she said again. She looked at him with startled green eyes, drawing in a quick breath, not knowing how to respond to his words. Was he really saying that he still wanted her? Surely he was just teasing…wasn't he?

Then he tugged on her arm and the moment dissolved into nothingness. 'This way,' he said. 'The living room is up here. I'll show you the layout and then I'll make us some coffee. I don't know about you but I'm parched.'

She was, too, she realised, especially since he had cast his grey eyes over her in that oddly fervent way. Her senses were working overtime, and her heart was racing as though she had run a mile.

He showed her into the living room. It was stunning, a large, spacious room full of natural light, and once again she found herself staring around, open-mouthed.

Long corner settees were arranged at either side of the room, providing seating near large windows. They were upholstered in a rich, creamy fabric, with cushions lending colour and warmth. There was a low glass table, and to one side there was a shelving unit displaying delicately fashioned ceramics and glassware that reflected the sun's rays.

'This is so lovely,' she breathed. 'It's all so simple and uncluttered, and everything is just perfect.' Her gaze went to the far end of the room, where there was a dining area, leading to a breakfast kitchen.

The lines of the kitchen were clean and sleek, with chrome and smoked-glass surfaces and a range of units that included wall-mounted cupboards with glass fronts.

'I can't believe you ever do any cooking in

here,' she said. 'It's all so sparkling and fresh, with nothing out of place.'

His mouth twisted a fraction. 'I do tend to eat a lot of my meals at the hospital, and I have to admit that I phone out for take-aways quite a bit. It suits me. I'm usually too busy to be bothered with cooking.'

'I know the feeling, but with Connor to take care of, I have to make sure that we have good, wholesome food.'

She glanced around and walked into the breakfast area, where light streamed in through a wide expanse of windows on either side of French doors. 'This is heavenly, though, a dream kitchen, and you even have doors that open out onto the terrace.' It was fashioned like a small courtyard out there, with planters containing feathery leaved ornamental trees and foliage plants that made it all seem like a little gem of countryside set in the middle of the City.

'I was quite taken with the place when I first saw it. It isn't all that big, but it serves my purposes and I've felt good about living here. I'm not sure what I'll do with it when it becomes time to move on.'

Allison felt a pang of dismay at the thought of him leaving. She had wondered if he might decide to stay, to look for a post within the same hospital, or at one nearby, when this contract ended. His words made it sound so final, as though he was already planning ahead.

He had started to make coffee, laying a tray with crockery, cream and sugar, and now he added a platter, which he filled with a selection of nibbles, small sandwiches, cheese and biscuits, grapes and alongside that a small bowl of salad.

'We could take this outside,' he suggested, and she nodded, following him out onto the terrace with the coffee-pot and serviettes and placing them down on to a wrought-iron table.

They sat down, and Taylor began to pour coffee for both of them. 'I like to come out here and just sit and think for a while sometimes,' he said. 'It's pleasant in the warmth of the afternoon and evening.'

'Yes, it is.' She glanced around and saw that they were screened from view out here by a wall of greenery. 'You could probably sit here and forget the troubles of the day for a while.'

They polished off the food and drank coffee, reminiscing about old times and bringing to mind people they knew from their old haunts, until Taylor asked, 'Would you like something stronger to drink...a glass of wine, perhaps, or a liqueur? You aren't driving, so it won't matter, will it?'

She sent him a long, guarded look. 'I don't think I'd better,' she murmured. 'I have to get back home to see to Connor.'

'Can't I tempt you to try just one?'

She shook her head. 'That wouldn't be very wise. I made that mistake once before. It started with just one, and then there was another, and before I knew it things were getting out of hand. I don't think I'll go down that route again. You know what they say, don't you? Once bitten, twice shy.'

A smile touched his mouth. 'It was just an innocent suggestion, I promise. I really didn't have an ulterior motive, honestly. Neither did I before, except that I wanted to get you warmed up after your foray into the cold. Your teeth were chattering and I was worried about you.'

'Yes, well...I think I'll leave well alone, if

it's all the same to you. I'm feeling too laid back already, and I still have to go home.'

He stood up and came over to her, bending towards her and dropping a kiss on her cheek. It was a totally unexpected gesture, and her whole body sizzled in reaction, the blood starting to run through her veins in a sudden surge of activity. 'I'm glad that you've been able to relax,' he said softly.

She stared up at him, her mouth dropping open a fraction, and he looked at her, his gaze sliding down to trace the fullness of her pink lips, his eyes taking on a smoky hue.

'Irresistible,' he said on a sigh, and then he was kissing her, his mouth capturing hers and gently savouring its sweet softness.

Allison's mind went into a spin, her thoughts spiralling out of control. Her lips clung to his, her body responding in full measure to the way his hands were lightly caressing her, revelling in the touch that had been denied her for so long.

The kiss deepened as he moved in closer to explore the softness of her mouth. His palm swept upwards, his thumb gently nudging her breast so that the nub hardened, and she felt the breath suddenly constrict in her lungs. Her eyes widened and her body arched slightly.

Wasn't this what she had wanted, yearned for ever since she had left his house in Buckinghamshire all that time ago? And here she was once more, in his apartment, in his arms, loving the way that he was kissing her and gently running his hands over her soft curves.

How was it that he was able to entice her into behaving in such a reckless fashion? Hadn't she already paid too high a price for what had happened before? Her child was her life, but where was his father's love and promise of commitment?

The thought winged its way into her head out of nowhere, and she must have stiffened because he seemed to sense her reluctant with-drawal from him.

'I'm sorry,' he said, pulling back after a moment or two of hesitation and giving a small shake of his head. 'I shouldn't have done that. I don't know what came over me.' He winced. 'Maybe it's that you looked so vulnerable earlier, and we've only just had a chance to talk properly for the first time in ages. Perhaps it was just that old times came rushing to the fore and swept any common sense out of my head.'

She came back down to earth with a bump. 'It's all right,' she said, her voice husky. 'It's been an odd sort of day. I wasn't thinking properly, either.'

Her mind was still in a whirl. All this time, and nothing had changed. His kisses were as potent as ever, and it was only now dawning on her that what had happened so long ago had been much more than just an act of fate. She could have stopped it before things had got out of hand, but the truth was, she had desperately wanted him back then, and her need for him had never gone away.

She said, 'I should go back home and see if Connor is all right. We're expecting Nick to drop in on us later on, and I need to be there.'

'I'll take you,' Taylor said.

'Thanks.' She told herself that it was good that the moment had passed. She had to put Taylor out of her mind, once and for all, because there was never going to be an opportunity for them to get together in the way that she would have liked. The obstacles that had lain in her path five years ago were still firmly in place. None of them had fallen by the wayside.

He had said and done nothing that would make her feel that he was ready to welcome a child into his life and, in fact, looking around this apartment, she had to ask herself how on earth a little boy would fit into his bachelor existence.

All this time she had kept her silence, afraid that he wouldn't want to acknowledge his son, and her reasoning for that was still sound, wasn't it? He was still on the move, preparing to leave for pastures new at some point in the future, and where would that leave any relationship he might have with Connor?

And, added to all of that, wasn't there the constant worry about the role he had played in her brother's downfall? How could she care anything at all for a man who could destroy someone in her family? Where was her loyalty?

CHAPTER SIX

'WOULD it be all right with you if I was to store these costumes in a corner of the living room?' Rhea asked, waving a hand over a large cardboard box that Nick was carrying for her. It was about the size of a packing crate. 'I know it's a nuisance, and I hate to be so disruptive, but we keep tripping over it in the bedroom.'

'It's not your fault,' Allison said with a frown, 'and anyway things haven't worked out too badly so far, have they?'

Rhea and Poppy had been staying with her for a couple of weeks now, and so far it was all going smoothly enough. It was a small house, though, and they were bound to get under each other's feet from time to time. There were only two bedrooms, and the biggest problem was that they'd had to bring a camp bed into each room for the children.

'Perhaps you could put the costumes in the dining area by the table,' she said now. 'That way, they will be close by where you set up your sewing machine. I know it's awkward, having to put it away every time we have a meal, but I can't think of an alternative at the moment.'

'Bless you,' Rhea murmured.

Nick put down the box and pushed it into a corner. 'You girls seem to be getting along well enough, at any rate, for all that you're crowded together here. Perhaps it's because you're both fairly tolerant people by nature.'

He glanced at Allison. 'Can you imagine how Mum and Dad would have reacted under the circumstances? They both had a short fuse, and they'd have been at each other's throats from the sheer frustration of being cooped up together in such a small space. I don't know how you and I managed to miss out on the gene bank on that score.'

Allison gave a wry smile. 'Don't knock it. Anyway, I don't believe it was a question of missing out. I think we saw so many arguments at home that we decided to do away with them in our own lives.'

In fact, her life at home had coloured her thinking about relationships in general. She wasn't at all sure that she would ever want to be so close to any man that she might trust him with her heart and soul. There was always the risk that everything would fall apart, the way her parents' marriage had slowly disintegrated.

She said quietly, 'Besides, Rhea and I have always been great friends.'

Rhea was still concerned. 'I feel bad that we're taking up so much of your living space, but I couldn't face the thought of going back to my house with Steve hanging around there. I tried to go home to collect some more things the other day, but he was prowling around and I drove straight by without stopping.'

'It's really difficult for you, isn't it?' Allison was sympathetic. 'Is there any chance that he might have found a job? At least that would keep him occupied for part of the day and it might give you more of a chance to collect what you need.'

'Yes, I saw him getting into the driver's seat of a delivery van that was parked nearby, and it occurred to me that he might have started to work regular hours. I made up my mind that I'd have another go tomorrow at fetching some things from the house. There's a good chance that he only comes around to my place when he's on a lunch-break, so I'll choose my time with that in mind.'

'Whatever you do, be careful.' Allison was busy clearing up some of Connor's toys, while he was quietly drawing a picture at the table. At first he had been lending a helping hand, but he kept discovering things that he wanted to play with, and time was getting on. Allison wanted the place cleared up for suppertime.

She glanced at her brother. 'Couldn't you spare Ben to go with Rhea?'

'I would, but the auditors are coming in, and we both have a meeting with the accountant tomorrow. I could sort something out for later on in the day, or we could arrange something for the day after tomorrow.'

Rhea shook her head. 'Thanks, but I want to

do it while Poppy's spending some time at her father's house. It will be the ideal opportunity for me. That way, I'll only have one little person tugging at my jeans pocket.' She sent a quick grin in Connor's direction. 'I'll pick him up from school and take him with me.' Glancing at Allison, she said, 'I don't know how long I'll be there—maybe an hour or so.'

Allison nodded. 'Just keep a lookout for trouble.' She went into the kitchen and started to serve up the supper, while Rhea and Nick detached Connor from his drawing and began to lay the table. 'You can help,' she heard Rhea say to Connor. 'See if you can set out the cutlery for us.'

The doorbell rang as Allison was setting out dishes of steaming vegetables and spicy hotpot on the table. Rhea went to answer it, and a moment later Taylor walked into the room.

'I'm sorry. I didn't mean to disturb your meal,' he said, flicking his gaze over the appetising spread. He started to turn away. 'I'll come back another day.'

'No, don't do that.' Allison intervened quickly.

'Stay and have some food with us. I'll get another plate. There's plenty for everyone.'

'If you're sure?'

He looked doubtful, but Connor said on a bright note, 'It'll be all right. If you don't like it, you don't have to eat it. If I leave my dinner, my mummy doesn't say anything. She just takes it away. It's only if you say yuck that she gets cross, and then she makes you try a bit.'

Taylor's mouth crinkled at the corners. 'I'll try to remember that. Never say yuck about your mother's cooking.'

They all sat down to eat just a moment or so later, and generally there was a cheerful atmosphere around the table. It was only Nick who was quiet and withdrawn, and Allison caught a sombre expression in his eyes whenever he glanced towards Taylor.

Taylor must have been well aware of Nick's restrained hostility, but he said nothing in that regard, but instead outlined the details of a property that he had found for Rhea.

'Are you still thinking about moving out of your house for good?' he asked, and Rhea nodded.

'I've been to the police, as you suggested, but they can't do anything more than slap an injunction on Steve, unless he actually physically harms me.' She kept her voice low, so that Connor wouldn't take note of what she was saying. 'The truth is, I think he's obsessed, and nothing will stop him, short of him being locked up in prison.'

'Well, in that case, you might want to take a look at the house I have in mind. It's in the same catchment area for the school, but it's also fairly close to the local police station. It isn't very big…there's just one double bedroom and a smaller single room, which I imagine will be just about adequate for Poppy, but the reception room is quite large, and there's a separate dining kitchen. You don't have to accept it, of course, but if you do, it will tide you over for as long as you need it.'

'When will it be ready?' She speared vegetables with her fork.

'Not for a couple of days. The decorators are working on it at the moment, but as soon as they've finished we can move you in there.'

'Oh, that's great news. Thanks, Taylor. That's good to know.' She sent Allison a quick grin. 'You'll be able to have your house to yourself again…and Poppy will be so excited.'

Taylor sampled the meat on his plate, and seemed to appreciate the flavour, so much so that he took another enthusiastic bite. 'Take a look at the property before you make any decisions,' he cautioned Rhea after a moment or two. 'You might not like it, and I imagine Poppy will have something to say about the place you choose.'

'I'm sure she'll love it if I'm happy with it, but thanks again.'

'Poppy isn't here,' Connor piped up in an earnest voice, looking at Taylor. He was holding a fork in his fist, gesturing with his forearm as he spoke, and the potato on the end of the prongs made a spiral journey through the air. 'She's gone to stay with her daddy.'

'Has she? That must be nice for her.' Taylor looked at him thoughtfully, as though he was studying his features, and Allison experienced a small frisson of anxiety. Would he recognise that this child was his son?

'Do you miss her when she isn't here?' Taylor asked.

Connor nodded. 'Yes, I do, because we play Mums and Dads together.' He put down his fork and frowned, his mouth jutting in a belligerent fashion. 'I don't see why she has a daddy and I don't. The children at school have daddies.'

'Do they? All of them?'

Allison caught her breath. This was the first time that Connor had expressed his feelings in this way, and she couldn't help but feel anxious about what was going on in his head.

Connor mused on that. 'Well, mostly they do.' He screwed up his eyes and bunched up his knees, so that his feet were on the seat of his chair. 'I want a daddy, because I want to play at fighting and go motorbike racing and a daddy would buy me a big yellow racing car what I can sit in.' He glowered at Allison. 'Mummy won't buy me one. She says I have to wait and see what Santa brings me, and that's not going to be for a long time, is it? Not for ages.' He spread his arms wide as though to demonstrate the enormity of that expanse of time.

'Well, I can see how that might be a problem,' Taylor said, tilting his head on one side and looking closely at Connor. 'Boys need their cars, don't they?'

'Yes, they do.' Connor's head nodded vigorously.

Taylor sent a fleeting glance in Allison's direction, and then turned his attention back to her little boy. 'I know it seems like a long while, but you might not have to wait until Christmas time to be able to enjoy yourself. There are some places where you can go and ride on the play equipment, just like you do sometimes at school, perhaps—there may not be a yellow car, but I know a farm where you can ride on pedal tractors. That might be a lot more exciting than just sitting in a car.'

Connor's eyes widened. 'Tractors?' he said, his interest tweaked. Then he asked, 'Can you ride on real tractors?'

Taylor nodded. 'You might be able to sit on one, as long as it's not moving, but I know they do trailer rides, where the tractor pulls you along.'

Connor looked at him curiously. 'How do you know?'

'My sister has two little boys, Adam and Josh—they're a bit older than you, but she takes them out to visit a farm sometimes, and they really like it there. There are lots of animals to see, and there's an adventure playground where they can climb on things. They have a lot of fun when they go there.'

'Do they? Will you take me there?'

Taylor's mouth stayed open for a second or two as he realised what he had just walked into. 'I, um…I think that would depend on what your mother has to say about it.'

'She won't mind. She lets me go places with Rhea.' Connor looked at Allison. 'Can I go, Mum?'

Allison gave it some thought. 'We'll see. If I get the weekend off work and the weather is fine, I might take you.'

'But I want to go with him.' Connor waved a hand in Taylor's direction.

Taylor smiled wryly. 'What about your mother? What will she do if you go to the farm with me?'

'Oh, that's all right. She can come, as well.'

Taylor chuckled, and Allison tried to hide a

JOANNA NEIL

smile. 'Well, I'm glad about that,' she told Connor. 'I thought perhaps you were going to leave me at home.'

'Nah…I wouldn't do that,' Connor said. 'Can I go and play with my toys now?'

'If you've finished eating, yes.'

Connor slid down from the table and went to rummage through his toy box.

Rhea almost choked on her coffee. She was trying not to laugh, and Nick slapped her on the back in order to help her recover. When she had finished spluttering, she said, 'Well, Taylor, that will teach you not to put ideas into Connor's head. You might not have promised to take him but he'll keep on reminding you from time to time. He never forgets anything.'

'I'm beginning to realise that,' Taylor said. 'I can see I shall have to watch my step from now on.'

They sat and talked for a while longer, but then Nick excused himself, saying, 'I'd better go. I have to prepare for the auditors tomorrow.'

'Are you expecting things to go well?' Taylor asked.

Nick hesitated. 'We've nothing to hide, and as

far as I know everything is in order. It's taken us a long while to get back on our feet, but I think we're getting there at last.' He didn't exactly say that Taylor had been to blame for what had happened in the past, but his eyes were dark, his expression bleak, and Allison was sure that Taylor received the message loud and clear.

'So you're not expecting a rerun of the problems you had before?'

Nick's eyes narrowed. 'No, we aren't.'

Allison knew what he was thinking. Although he had never said anything before this, Taylor must have known all along that the company had been the subject of a police investigation in the past. Did he know the full extent of it, that it had involved a problem with identity theft and fraudulent dealings? No evidence of their involvement had been put forward, and that had been why they had been able to start up again in business. Was it possible that he thought her brother had been responsible? Or maybe he blamed Ben?

She felt awkward about the tension between the two men, but she didn't know what she could do to make things right. One was her brother and the other her boss, the father of her child, and she was caught between the two of them.

'You've always had a good product,' Taylor remarked. 'There was never anything wrong with your designs or your workmanship. I hope things turn out all right for you.'

'Thank you.' Nick's mouth was set in a straight line. He went and said goodbye to Rhea and made his way to the door.

'I'll see you out,' Allison murmured, going with him.

When they were alone, she said softly, 'I know it must have been awkward for you, having Taylor stay for dinner with us. I could hardly turn him away, though, could I, especially when he's helping Rhea?'

'I know. I understand.' Nick gave her a long look. 'I'm not the only one who has a problem with Taylor, though, am I? You haven't told him that he's Connor's father, have you?'

She shook her head. 'I can't bring myself to do it. For one thing, I don't know how long he's going to be staying around.'

'But you heard what Connor had to say. Sooner or later, he's going to start asking deeper, more searching questions about why he doesn't have a father. What are you going to tell him then?'

'I don't know.' She made a face. 'All I know is that I don't want him to be hurt. I don't want him to get to know his father and then have him move away, out of his life.'

'Taylor wouldn't necessarily have to get to know him or be part of his day-to-day life. Perhaps it would be enough for him to simply acknowledge that he had a son and make some sort of financial contribution to his welfare.'

'I doubt that he would see things that way. He would probably feel obliged to do more than just acknowledge him, but it wouldn't work out for any of us that way. Connor would grow up feeling resentful, and Taylor would feel trapped. He doesn't want children in his life. He said so. I'm sure he would be alarmed to discover that he had a child.'

'He might have changed his mind on that score. He seemed to be getting on well enough with Connor back there.' Nick jerked his head in the direction of the sitting room.

'I don't think a brief encounter qualifies as groundwork for parenting. He hasn't changed that much. You should see his apartment. It's pristine, untouched, and not at all the kind of place where you would want children to wander about unfettered. I know that he looked after his nephews recently, but he went to his sister's house to do that, and I don't think he was at all comfortable taking on the responsibility.'

Nick squeezed her arm. 'You know that I'll support you, whatever you decide to do. I'd just prefer it if Taylor and I don't have to meet too often.'

Allison waved him goodbye a short time later and went back into the living room. Rhea was clearing away the supper dishes, and Taylor was sitting with Connor, looking through his sketch-book and admiring the various squiggles that covered each page. He seemed to be faintly bemused by the experience, and Allison took pity on him and went to rescue him.

'He doesn't know what that is,' Connor said,

waving a page in front of her nose. A pencilled picture showed a vaguely rectangular shape that had several lines crossing through it. 'I told him it's a lorry.'

'Well, of course it is,' Allison agreed. She pointed with a finger. 'There's the cab with the window, and there's the driver at the front, see?' She looked at Taylor, shaking her head, sharing her son's incredulity. 'Anyone can see that it's a lorry.'

Taylor's brows rose. 'Ah, yes, of course it is. I see it now.' He smiled at the boy. 'I have to go now, Connor. I need to get on with a few things back at my apartment. Perhaps I'll see you again?'

Connor nodded. 'Bye.'

Taylor stood up and went with Allison to the door. 'There were no wheels,' he said in an undertone. 'How did you know what it was?'

'He was looking at pictures of lorries before he drew it. You have to use guesswork, or maybe ask a few subtle questions.' She sent him a quick grin. 'Never mind, you'll get the hang of it one day.'

He grimaced. 'I don't think so. Perhaps I'll pass on that one.' He glanced at her. 'Thanks for giving me supper. It was delicious… It seems as though it's a long time since I sat down to enjoy home cooking.' His gaze moved over her, and he looked as though he might have said more, but then he braced himself and said, 'I should go.'

Allison showed him out, watching him get into his car and take off down the road. She felt sad inside, because that was the crux of the matter really, wasn't it? He didn't want to get involved in the intricacies of being a parent, and in the end he would always be able to simply drive away.

She met up with him the next day in A and E, but there was little time to talk, because they were kept busy dealing with casualties from a road accident.

In a separate incident, later on in the afternoon, a woman in her fifties was brought in by ambulance after being involved in a car crash. Taylor was trying to fathom the extent of her injuries.

'She swerved to avoid an oncoming car,' he told Allison, 'and then she smashed into a tree at the side of the road. Her seat belt appears to have saved her from any major harm, but there's a lot of bruising and she's very shocked and distressed. Apart from cuts and grazes caused by broken glass, I can't see any external injuries. Something's wrong, though. She's complaining of abdominal pain, which must be pretty severe, judging by her response to my examination and by the way she feels the need to lie very still. Since she was brought in here she's been vomiting.'

'Her blood pressure is very low,' Allison said, 'and her temperature is rising. Do you want to do blood tests and an X-ray?'

'Yes, that would be a good idea.' He seemed faintly distracted, his gaze flicking to the corridor beyond the main floor of the A and E department. 'Would you mind taking over here for a moment?'

'No, that's OK.' She studied him briefly, wondering what might be causing his preoccupation. It wasn't at all like him to be like this. She didn't query it, though, and as he hurried away she set about organising the lab tests.

When the woman came back from X-Ray, Allison studied the films and saw that they showed an area of free gas under the diaphragm.

From the level of pain that the woman had to endure, she suspected that a CT scan would show a leakage of substances into the peritoneum.

'Mrs Walker, I'm going to give you morphine for the pain,' she murmured, 'and I'm going to add cyclizine, to stop you from being sick. Once you're feeling a little easier, perhaps we can talk and you can fill me in on some background details.'

Sarah came to assist after a while, and Allison put in a nasogastric tube. 'We'll give her saline, and I'm going to prepare an injection of antibiotics, cefuroxime and metronidazole. I want to send her for a CT scan, and then I think we need to ask for a surgeon to come down and take a look at her, so I'll go and organise all that now. Keep her on oxygen via a mask, will you, while I go and have a word with Taylor?'

'I will.'

Allison went in search of Taylor a few minutes later, and found him in the doctors' rest room. He wasn't alone. Two young boys, aged around six or seven, were there with him, one of them busily checking out all the cupboards in the room, while the other was applying a bandage to Taylor's ankle. That might not have been a problem, except that he was winding it around the leg of the chair near to where Taylor was standing.

'Are these your nephews?' she asked.

He nodded. 'That's right, for my sins. I'm expecting Claire to come and take them off my hands at any moment, but you know how it is with my sister. Things never seem to go according to plan.'

'Yes, I remember. She was always getting into scrapes of one kind or another.' Claire was ditzy, a lively, extrovert sort of person, hardly ever fazed by anything. She frowned, collecting herself. 'Can I have a word?'

'Sure.'

'It's about Mrs Walker. I think she has a perforated ulcer and the beginnings of peritonitis. I've arranged for the surgeon to come and look at her.'

'That's good. Did you do a CT scan?'

'She's going for that now. I've been talking to her and it looks as though there's a history of ulceration. Lately she's been going through a lot of stress, and I think the accident was the last straw.'

'You did well to pick up on the symptoms. Did you have some idea that it might be ulcers that were causing the trouble?'

She nodded. 'I remember how Nick was when the business folded. He lost a lot of money and things were really bad, and the stress started to get to him. He was in pain and he lost weight, and in the end he started to be sick a lot. He didn't really understand why things had gone wrong, and he wasn't sure how to handle it.'

Taylor looked at her steadily. 'Do you blame me for that?'

Allison moistened her lips with the tip of her tongue. 'Yes, I think I do, in part. You pulled the rug out from under his feet and added to his stress at a time when things were going downhill. Having to find new premises at short notice came as a real jolt to him. He had expected you to renew the lease, and when you didn't, he was suddenly catapulted into a whole new set-up. Premises weren't easy to find, and they were all far more expensive than he could afford. He started to lose orders because he couldn't fulfil his obligations to customers.'

'I don't believe I was entirely to blame for that. He was losing custom before I pulled the lease.'

'Maybe. At any rate, that's all in the past, and it's over now.' She didn't want to argue with him. After all, it had been his property to do with as he'd pleased, and it had been unfortunate that her brother and Ben had ended up as collateral damage. His actions had never really made sense to her. They hadn't fitted with her image of him, even less so now that he was helping Rhea.

He looked down at his young nephew. 'I think that's enough bandaging for now, Adam,' he murmured. 'I have to go and see to my patients.'

The boy took no notice at all and went on with the bandaging, starting on Taylor's other leg and binding that to the chair, too.

'Josh, come down from there.' Taylor frowned as the older boy climbed up onto the work surface and tried to explore the contents of the wall cabinet. Neither boy responded.

'I'm waiting,' he said, his tone sharp, so that this time both boys turned to look at him. 'Josh, get down from there this minute.' He turned towards Adam. 'As for you, young man, that will be quite enough first aid for now.' He took a pair of scissors from his pocket and cut through the bonds. 'Both of you, come over here and sit down at the table.'

He glowered at them when neither boy made a move. 'I'm not going to repeat myself.'

There must have been something in his manner that finally got through to them, because both boys suddenly decided it would be wise to do as they were told and slid into the seats. They waited while he freed himself from the coils of bandage.

He hunted in a drawer and then pushed a sheet of paper and pencils in front of each of them. 'Draw,' he said. 'Don't move from the spot until your mother comes back.'

Allison sent him a brief glance. 'Why is Claire here in the hospital?' she asked. 'Is she seeing a doctor?' She was worried for him all at once. He and his sister had always been close, despite their differences in temperament. 'Is she ill?'

He shook his head. 'That's just the point. Claire is never ill, but just lately she's been feeling nauseous and under the weather. She said she'd been throwing up some mornings, so she decided she wanted to come and have a word with a friend who works here.'

'Who is she seeing?'

'Mary, from upstairs. You know, the obs-gynae doctor? They're good friends.' He stopped suddenly, as though he had just realised what he had said, and his eyes widened.

His expression was so stunned that Allison couldn't help herself. She started to chuckle. 'Did it not dawn on you before this?'

He groaned. 'That's it, isn't it?' He lowered his voice. 'She must be pregnant. Why didn't I think of it?'

'Because you're her brother?'

'I suppose so.' He grimaced. 'She must be mad. What can have possessed her? You'd have thought she had enough on her hands with those two.'

'She may not have planned it,' Allison ventured. 'Accidents happen...even with the best of precautions.' She sent him a cautious look.

He stared at her. 'Is that what happened with you?' He lowered his voice so that the boys would not hear what he was saying. 'Ever since I discovered that you have a child, I haven't been able to get my head around it. You and I were as close as it's possible to be, and even though it was just the once that we came together, we were careful. You had just qualified as a doctor, and you had your whole career ahead of you, and I didn't want to take the chance of ruining any of that.'

He shook his head as though it was all beyond his understanding. 'And yet you must have changed your whole view of life just a short time afterwards. Why else would you take the risk of becoming pregnant? Was it that you fell for someone, or maybe you just decided that motherhood was what you wanted after all? Did something go wrong?'

She gave a faint, ironic smile. 'You could say that. Although, as it turns out, I've discovered that Connor is the most precious thing in my life, so I really don't have any regrets on that score.'

Taylor was silent for a moment, but then he placed his hands on her upper arms, drawing her towards him. His hold on her was gentle but firm, as though he would keep her near him and protect her from harm. 'It must have been hard for you, going through all that alone. I don't understand why you didn't tell Connor about his father, and I've been thinking it through. It couldn't have been Ben, could it? He's a normal, decent sort of man, and I don't see how you would have stayed close to him all this time and not become a family unit.'

'Does it matter?' she said. 'It was all a long time ago, and I made a mistake. I wasn't going to see Connor's father again and I didn't want to compound that mistake by involving anyone else in my problems.'

He frowned, looking into her eyes, and just then the door to the rest room opened and his sister walked in.

Taylor let go of Allison and she was very still for a moment or two, trying to absorb the fact that he was no longer holding her close, and doing her best to calm the hammering of her heart. She didn't know why he had this effect on her, but whenever he was near he made her want what she couldn't have.

'Hi,' Claire said. 'I'm back. You wouldn't believe the number of people who are still waiting to be seen in the clinic upstairs.' Her black hair was tousled, a mass of cloudy curls that tumbled over her shoulders and rippled as she advanced into the room. Her gaze went to the table where the boys were sitting.

'Has everything been all right while I've been gone?' Claire looked at her sons. 'You're both suspiciously quiet. Have you been behaving yourselves?'

The boys made noncommittal sounds, making out that they were engrossed in their drawing. She accepted that at face value and turned to look at Allison. 'Hello, Allie,' she said. 'It's been ages since we've seen each other, hasn't it? Has my brother been looking after you? I couldn't believe it when he said you were working together.'

Allison tried on a smile. 'It's a funny old world, isn't it? It's good to see you again, Claire.'

The moment with Taylor was lost for ever by the intrusion, and she didn't know whether she was sad about that or relieved.

CHAPTER SEVEN

'HAS Claire gone home already?' Allison asked, stopping by the treatment bay where Taylor was busy checking a patient's ECG results.

Seeing his long, lean figure made her heart slip into an erratic rhythm all over again, and it unnerved her that he should have this effect on her. She was still remembering the thrill of having him hold her close and more than anything she wanted to know what it was that he felt for her. He seemed to care for her, and even want her, but was there anything more than that? Her own feelings were thoroughly mixed up. Was this love that she felt for him, this feeling of wanting to be close to him all the time?

He looked up from the ECG trace. 'Yes, she left here a few minutes ago. Why, did you want to speak to her?'

'No, it's just that I somehow expected her to stay around for a bit longer. I haven't seen her in ages and I thought we might have time to chat, seeing that I'm off duty now.'

Taylor glanced at the nurse who was assisting and said, 'The patient's heart rate is way too fast, but there's no abnormal rhythm, so we'll try her on a beta blocker to see if that will slow things down a bit. I'll prepare an injection first of all and see how that works out, and then maybe, if all's well, we'll follow up with tablets.'

He came to stand by the curtained entrance of the treatment room and glanced at Allison.

'I'm sure Claire would have stayed if she could, but she said she had to get back to make sure that her dog was all right. Apparently he's been cooped up for most of the day.'

'No problem. Perhaps I'll catch up with her some other time.' She sent him a quick look. 'Shouldn't you have been off duty some time ago? You were here before I was this morning.'

He nodded. 'There are just a few things I need to check up on before I do that.'

It didn't surprise her that he wasn't in any hurry

to leave. He put in long hours at the hospital, and even when he wasn't with patients, he was often busy sorting out changes that would, in the long run, make a significant difference to the general efficiency of the department.

'This place is like your second home, isn't it? Are you doing all this because you want to make your mark? You were always keen to get on, weren't you? But I would have thought now that you're a consultant you would be able to relax a little. Don't you ever feel the need to let go?'

He looked startled. 'Why would I? This is what I love to do, and I can't imagine what it would be like to be at work from nine to five each day. Besides, I have to think about what I want to do when this position closes. Where do I want to go from here?' He shrugged. 'I've been offered a place back in Hampshire, but it calls for extra administrative skills and I'm working all the while to achieve them. As it is, I'm lucky that I'm a free agent, and I don't ever have to worry about getting home on time.'

So he was definitely going to leave, eventually. The knowledge brought her spirits down with a sickening lurch. 'Doesn't that make you feel isolated sometimes? Don't you ever wonder what it would be like to be similar to your sister and have someone to go home to each day—a wife and family of your own, maybe? There must have been odd times when you've given it some thought.'

He was silent for a moment, his expression becoming serious. 'Maybe.' Taylor looked at her, his gaze shifting over her features, his eyes darkening to an intense shade of grey, so that she began to wonder if he might have taken exception to her question in some way.

But then he seemed to shrug off his sober mood, adding, 'But they certainly were odd times, when I think perhaps I might have suffered a mental lapse. It isn't going to happen.' He gave her a faint smile. 'Anyway, I only have to be with Claire and her brood for an hour or so, and I find myself longing for the peace and quiet of my apartment. Perhaps I'm not cut out for family life.'

She hadn't really expected any other kind of answer from him, had she? She might have hoped that he would express some need for closeness, but he wasn't about to declare that he had any deep feelings for her, was he? Their precious moments of togetherness belonged firmly in the past, a warm nugget of comfort tucked away deep inside her.

For her own part, she couldn't imagine dedicating her life simply to work, and perhaps he caught something of what she was thinking because he sent her an oddly searching look and commented, 'I expect you're only too glad to be able to go home and spend time with Connor.'

'Yes, that's true.'

He smiled. On a whim, he put out a hand and ran a finger lightly through the golden strands of her hair, tucking a stray curl behind her ear. 'I can see how strong the bond is between the two of you. He's lucky to have you,' he murmured. 'You seem to have things just about right.'

Allison nodded. 'Do I? I know that he can be a handful at times, but I love him dearly, and I do look forward to being with him. He brightens up my life.'

The thought popped into her mind that she

would like to spend time with Taylor, too, but she squashed that idea as soon as it came into being. What would be the point in hoping for that? There was no room for her in his life. He was dedicated to his job. It was everything to him, and the fact that he was only there to cover for the previous consultant seemed to make no difference to his approach to the work in hand. He was full of ideas as to how things could be improved.

'Perhaps I'll see you later, just as soon as I've finished work,' he said. 'I shouldn't be too much longer. I have to check up on my patient's medication, and make sure that it's slowing the heart rate down adequately, but once I'm sure that I can safely hand over to the registrar I'll be able to leave. I told Rhea that I would bring her a folder of details about the house, so that she could glance through them.'

'Did you? Yes, later, then.'

She dawdled although it was time for her to go home from work. Rhea would probably still be at her house, collecting the rest of her things, and there was really no need for her to rush about. There was no meal to organise, because they had planned on having a light supper, a salad, maybe, something that wouldn't take too much preparation.

The day was warm, and she felt restless for fresh air after the antiseptic smell of the hospital, so she collected her things together and decided to go for a walk.

She ended up in Regent's Park, where she sat for a while and watched waterfowl meander gracefully across the lake. Mother ducks gathered their broods about them, going off in search of food, and their offspring followed, darting here and there across the water.

Allison wondered what it would be like to be as serene and untroubled by everyday events as they were. Life seemed to be so simple for them, and yet for her it was full of pitfalls. Only that morning Connor had asked her, 'Do I have a daddy?' And she hadn't known how to answer him.

'Yes, you do,' she had said, after a moment of reflection, 'but he doesn't live with us.'

'Why not?'

'Because sometimes daddies live some-where else.'

That had seemed to satisfy him for the time being, but she knew that sooner or later he would start to ask more questions. It was something she was going to have to deal with.

By now the sun was low in the sky, casting its rays over the smooth surface of the water, and she decided that it was time to go. Rhea and Connor should be arriving home any time now, and she wanted to be there to greet them. She set off for the tube station and thought about her plans for the evening.

Taylor had said he would come over, and she realised that she was looking forward to seeing him outside work. Maybe she would even be able at last to find the right words to tell him that Connor was his son. She frowned. How would he react to that?

A while later, she pushed open the front door of her house and went into the hallway, looking to see if Connor was back already.

The place was strangely silent, though, and straight away she had the feeling that something was wrong. 'Rhea... Connor,' she called out. 'Where are you?'

A vase lay on its side on the hall table, and perhaps it was just that it had been blown over by a cool breeze that was wafting along the narrow corridor. That probably simply meant that someone had forgotten to close a window somewhere in the house.

She walked into the living room and came to a sudden halt in the doorway. Nothing was as it should be. An armchair was tipped over on its back on the other side of the room, as though someone had pushed it hard from behind, until it had crashed against the wall and then toppled over. Drawers had been ripped out from the bureau and had been tossed onto the floor, so that the contents had spilled out over the rug.

Alarmed by what she was seeing, Allison went into the kitchen and discovered that it was the same in there. Anything that had once been set out tidily on the work surfaces was now strewn across the tiled floor. Crockery was smashed, even the tea service that her mother had given to her, and Connor's favourite mug, the one with the teddy-bear picture, was in bits.

Her throat seemed to swell, causing an aching

sensation that made it hard to swallow. She knelt down and started to carefully pick up the fragments, one by one, cherishing each small piece, remembering how he would curl his fingers around the mug and look at her from over the top of it with smiling, bright eyes. Her hands were shaking. How could she let him come home to find this devastation?

Who could have done this? Tears stung her eyelids, but she dashed them away with the back of her hand and stared about her. Whoever it had been must have come in through the window. The glass was shattered, covering the sink unit. That would account for the cool air that was even now wafting through the house.

'Allison?' Taylor's voice sounded far away. 'You left the front door open, so I came in. What's happened here?'

She turned to look up at him. Vaguely, she registered that he had changed out of his work clothes into casual chinos and a mid-blue shirt, but she had no idea what he was doing there right now. Then she guessed that time must have been moving on faster than she'd realised, and wondered how long it was she had been staring at the ruins of her home.

'I don't know.' Her voice was barely more than a whisper.

His gaze shifted over her, his eyes narrowing, and she looked down and discovered that she was still holding on to what was left of the mug. She stared down at her fingers and saw that blood was dripping from her palm onto the floor.

'You've cut yourself,' Taylor said. 'Here, let me help you with that.'

'This was Connor's,' she told him in a thready voice, holding out the remains of the ceramic mug. 'What am I going to say to him? How can I tell him that someone broke it? He won't be able to understand that.'

'Don't worry about it now.' Gently, but with a firm grasp on her arms, he drew her to her feet. 'Is the bathroom upstairs? Show me where you keep your first-aid box.'

She must have gone with him up the stairs, but she had no recollection of doing that. He sat her down by the side of the washbasin and bathed her palm, checking to see if there were any shards of pottery or glass embedded in the gash.

'It's quite a deep cut,' he said, 'but I think we can get away without putting a stitch in there. Perhaps I'll try a butterfly plaster. I'll dress it for you and that should make you feel more comfortable.'

She was silent while he tended to her, and perhaps that was because she was shocked by what had happened and too upset to take it all in. His hands were soothing, though, as he put the dressing in place, and every move he made was calm, confident and assured, so that she felt she could sit back for a moment and allow him to take over.

'Does that feel better?' he asked, when he had finished.

She nodded. 'Thanks.' Then she frowned, looking up at him. 'Connor should have been home by now,' she said, her throat strained. 'It must be getting late. Why isn't he here? And where's Rhea?' A sudden thought struck her and fear shivered along her spine. 'They were going to her house to collect some of her belongings.' Her eyes widened and she reached out and tugged on his shirtsleeve. 'I have to go. I have to go and see what's happened to them.'

'I'm way ahead of you.' His expression was serious. 'Are you sure that you're up to this? I could drop you off at my sister's house so that she can look after you. I'll go in your place to try and sort out any problem, if you want.'

'No. I need to be there. I need to know what's going on.' She was adamant. There was no way she was going to stay behind.

He seemed a little disturbed by her insistence on making the journey to the house, and she started to wonder what it was that was exercising his mind. Did he know more than he was letting on?

He stayed close-lipped, though, as he drove them to the house in Maida Vale, where Rhea lived, except to say as they drew close, 'I should tell you, Allison…I think Steve is at the house, but you must try not to worry. The police have been called and I'm sure they'll soon get the situation under control.'

Her eyes widened. 'How long has this been going on?'

He glanced down at his watch. 'A few hours.'

'A few hours?' She stared at him. All this time he had known that something was wrong, and yet he had kept it to himself. She was too alarmed right now to berate him about that. So many questions flooded into her mind. What was this situation that he had talked about? Was her little boy in danger? What about Rhea?

Even though he had told her something of what to expect, Allison wasn't prepared for the sight that met them when he eventually parked the car in Rhea's street. Rhea's house was cordoned off, and there were police everywhere. She saw, with a shudder, that they were armed with guns.

She looked out of the window, trying to take it all in. Neither of them made any attempt to get out of the car. She glanced at Taylor. 'How long have you known about this?' she asked.

'I heard something on the news when I left the hospital, so I made a few phone calls. I was hoping that it would all be over by the time we arrived here.'

'Have they said that it's Steve? How do they know that he's in the house?'

He nodded. 'A neighbour saw what was happening, and called the police. He said that Rhea was coming out of the house when Steve arrived, and he made her go back inside. He was worried because Rhea was clearly unhappy about going with him.'

'And Connor?' Her voice dropped to a cracked whisper. 'Is he with them?'

'Yes, he is. They managed to talk to officers briefly on the phone, so we know they're both safe, but no one can get to them at the moment. When the police arrived they discovered that Steve had barricaded the doors. I think they're taking things slowly. They don't want to rush in…' He broke off.

'Because they're afraid he might do something foolish… that's what you were going to say, weren't you?'

'I don't want you to be upset.'

'It's too late for that,' Allison said, tight-lipped. 'How else would I be, knowing that my son and my friend are locked inside a house with a madman?' Another, more worrying thought came into her mind. 'Why are the police carrying guns? Does Steve have a weapon?'

'I believe so.'

She looked at him, reading the darkness in his eyes. 'You're not telling me the full story, are you? Stop trying to protect me. What was it that he had—was it a knife? That seems to be about his calibre.'

Taylor nodded and moved to put an arm about her shoulders. 'Yes, it was. The neighbour said he saw him threatening her with it. The police have set up a support team with people specially trained to deal with this sort of thing. They were talking about bringing someone in to negotiate with him.'

'I can't imagine who would be able to do that. Rhea has been trying to talk to him for years without any result.'

'I know that. I spoke to the officer in charge, and tried to tell him what I knew of Steve's character. They'll use any scrap of information that they have in order to calm him down.'

'What kind of thing has he been saying?'

Taylor grimaced. 'Just the usual kind of thing. He wants Rhea to himself. He's obsessed with her. He's not going to let anyone near.'

Allison pushed open the door of the car and climbed out. 'We'll see about that. I'm going to try to find out what's happening,' she said. 'I need to know that Connor is safe. If he isn't, I'm going in there myself.'

Taylor went with her to find the policeman who was running the operation. In fact, she had the feeling that he wasn't going to let her out of his sight for an instant.

The man she spoke to was in his late fifties, an experienced officer, and he did what he could to soothe Allison's nerves, but she was very distressed and her mind kept going back to Connor. In the end, someone took her to one side so that she could give them a profile of Rhea's ex. Allison was reluctant to leave the vicinity of the house, but they persuaded her to go into a nearby community hall that had been commandeered for a short time as a temporary headquarters.

'It'll be better in here,' the officer told her. 'We can talk more easily and obtain a fuller picture of what it is we're dealing with.'

Allison told them all that she knew. Taylor

seemed to have disappeared somewhere along the way, and that was making her nervous on top of everything else. Why wasn't he there with her? She needed him by her side. If he wasn't there, she didn't seem to be able to function properly.

'I want to go outside and see if there's any way I can talk to my little boy and my friend,' she said, after a while, getting to her feet and walking over to the door. 'I need to hear his voice. I need to know that he's all right.'

'I don't know how close we can get,' the sergeant said, following her as she went outside. 'Your doctor friend has gone in to talk to the man, and we don't want to tip the balance and cause any sudden upsets.'

'Are you saying that he's actually inside the house?' Allison was horrified. 'How could you let him do that? He doesn't know Steve as well as Rhea and I do. The man has a knife. Anything could happen to him.'

'We made sure that he's wearing a protective jacket, and our people seem to think that the doctor can make a difference. Our profiler has talked to him and advised him how to handle the situation. With any luck, he'll be able to bring him out before too long.'

'How did he manage to get in there?'

'He spoke to Steve for a while by phone, and told him he was worried about the boy. He kept things very calm. We think he was allowed in so that he could check up on the child. The lad wasn't really crying, but he was sort of hiccuping a little bit every now and again, and it seemed to be distracting the man.'

Connor was obviously upset, and that knowledge made Allison more on edge than ever. Would Steve do anything to harm him? She was desperately worried about Taylor, too, but if there was any chance that he could bring Rhea and Connor out safely, perhaps his being in there was worth a try. But what if he was injured? It didn't bear thinking about.

Her mind was going round in circles, turning over each eventuality.

'Something's happening,' the sergeant said. 'The door's opening.'

Allison held her breath as the front door edged open. The police marksmen took aim and she wanted to shout out to them, Don't shoot…that might be my son who's coming out. Please, don't shoot.

Connor stood on the doorstep, a forlorn little figure, a bewildered four-year-old who had found himself caught up in a nightmare. Allison started forward and was held back in an iron grip by the police sergeant.

'Let our people go to him. You'll be able to see him in a little while, I promise.'

A woman officer hurried over to Connor and wrapped him in a blanket. Then she picked him up and moved away swiftly, heading towards the community hall. Allison went to follow, and this time the sergeant let her go. She glanced back at the house, seeing that the door was now firmly shut. What was going on in there? Was Rhea safe? And Taylor… What would become of him?

Connor needed her right now, though, and he had to be her main priority. She ran over to the hall where he was still in the arms of the policewoman, who was trying to comfort him. He looked up as Allison hurried into the room and he put out his arms to her, his lower lip starting to tremble.

'It was the bad man, Mummy. He pushed Rhea and he made me stay in the house. He wouldn't let me come out and I was scared.' The trembling worsened. 'I tried not to cry.'

'I know, sweetheart, I know. It must have been horrible for you, but you're safe now. I'm here. I have you safe.' He was shaking, and Allison wrapped her arms around him, lifting him and carrying him over to a chair. She sat down and held him on her lap, stroking his hair and whispering words of comfort until the tremors stopped and only an occasional sob sounded in the back of his throat.

She was terrified that something might have happened to Rhea or Taylor. 'Is there any news?' she asked the policewoman. 'Please, tell me what's happening.'

'It's not very clear. I think the doctor is trying to talk the man into giving himself up.'

'But what about Rhea? Is she hurt?'

Connor stirred in her arms. 'She hurted her wrist when the bad man pushed her over. She told him she thinks he broked it, but he didn't care. He just kept on shouting. Then the doctor man came and said something to him and made him be quiet. He put a bandage on her wrist and tried to make it better.'

Allison wrapped her arms more firmly around her little boy. She wasn't going to let him out of her sight now that she had him back with her. All she could do was to keep watch on the house through the window by her chair, and hope that Taylor could use his powers of persuasion to coax Steve into letting Rhea go free.

There was a sudden noise from outside, lots of shouting starting up and the sound of men running. She stiffened, looking at the police-woman in alarm. 'What is it? What's going on?' She could see the officers changing position outside, moving in closer to the house.

'Some of our men have gone in around the back of the house. They must have gained access through a roof space shared with the house next door. There was some covering noise set up to allow them to slip through, and the plan was to go from there through the loft and take him by surprise in the downstairs reception room.'

'Did the doctor know about the plan?'

The policewoman nodded. 'Once we had the child safe, that was the next stage of the operation. We couldn't leave him in there indefinitely because of the knife.'

It was all over in the next few minutes. Rhea came out first, a blanket around her shoulders, and Allison stood up, still holding on to her son, ready to go to her friend.

'May I go and see her?'

'Just for a moment, perhaps. They'll be taking her to the ambulance.'

As Allison walked outside, keeping Connor safe in her arms, she saw that an ambulance had been driven into the street, and its doors were open, ready to receive anyone who was injured.

Connor buried his head in the hollow of her shoulder, and she cradled him to her, stroking his silky black hair with her free hand.

'Rhea,' she said. 'I'm so sorry. I wish I could have done something to keep you safe. How badly are you hurt? Is Taylor all right?' She could see that Rhea's hand and forearm were supported by a makeshift sling.

Rhea was pale, and Allison could see that she

was shaken by her ordeal, but she managed to say, 'I'm OK. I'm just glad to be out of there.' She looked back at the house. 'I don't think I ever want to go back to that place. Perhaps I might go and visit with my parents for a while. They're always asking me to go and see them for longer than just a few hours.'

She gave a small shudder. 'I ought to have known Steve would catch up with me.' Her eyes closed briefly, as though she was trying to shut out the memory. 'I think Taylor will be out in a moment. I was so relieved when he persuaded Steve to let Connor go free. He seems to be fine, except for a bang on the head where Steve thumped him when the police rushed in. I just can't believe how cool he was in there, how he handled the situation. I was so glad to have him there with me.'

She paused, gathering her breath, as though she needed to get herself under control. 'As to all this, there was nothing you could do. It's all my fault. Nick rang and said he would come with me if I waited till later in the afternoon, but I was too impatient to do that. I thought I would be all right.'

Allison pressed her lips together. 'Is your wrist broken?' Despite what Rhea had said to the contrary, she was riddled with guilt about the whole episode. She ought to have done something to stop her from going to the house that day but, by keeping quiet, she had allowed Rhea and her own son to be endangered.

'Taylor says it is, most likely. He said it looked like a scaphoid fracture, whatever that is, but it doesn't feel too bad at the moment. He's given me something for the pain, and he says I'll need to go to the hospital to have a cast put on it.'

The paramedic came to help Rhea into the ambulance, and Allison debated whether she should go with her. Taylor was just coming out of the house, and she said quickly, 'I'll follow you to the hospital. I just need to make sure that Taylor is all right.'

'That's OK. Don't worry.'

Taylor glanced around, and Allison wondered if he was looking for Rhea. She hurried over to him. 'Are you all right? I was so worried when they told me what you were doing.'

'I'm fine.' He looked at Connor, who was

clinging on to her and keeping his face buried in her cotton top. 'How's this little fellow?'

'He's upset and baffled by everything that's been going on. Thank you for helping to get him out of there.' She looked at Taylor closely. 'Are you sure you're all right? Rhea said that Steve hit you.'

'He thought that I had tricked him when the police rushed in, and he lashed out when my guard was down. I was trying to be on the level with him, but he was very worked up. Luckily, I managed to grab hold of him and stop him from doing any more damage, and then the police took over.'

Allison was thoughtful. 'Do you think he went to my place first?'

Taylor nodded. 'I think he must have discovered where Rhea was staying. It can't have done much to calm his temper when he found that she wasn't there. That perhaps accounts for the mess. He must have gone straight round to her house after that.'

She winced. 'He's never acted in such an extreme way before. I can't imagine what possessed him to barricade himself in the house that way.'

Taylor grimaced. 'He seemed to have the idea that Rhea had a son.' His gaze met hers over the top of Connor's head, and she knew that he was trying to be careful in what he said. 'He was in a rage, but somehow Rhea managed to calm him down. I think she was doing her best to protect Connor as much as anything else.'

He kept his voice low. 'She sent Connor to go and play in the utility room so that he wouldn't see too much of what was going on. She probably thought it would be less challenging if he was out of sight.' Again, he glanced at Connor. 'I don't think he did very much in the way of playing. He's a bright boy, and he seemed to have been listening the whole time and taking everything in.'

'He does that. I'm going to have to be extra-careful with him over the next few weeks. He won't forget this in a hurry.'

'Have you decided what you're going to do now? I wouldn't have thought it would be a good idea for you to go back to the house. That might be another shock for him. Besides, the police will want to investigate to see if there's any evidence that Steve was the one who broke in.'

'I suppose you're right.' She made a face. 'I'll have to give it some thought, because there's Rhea to think of, too. I doubt she'll want to be on her own in her house after what's happened. Right now, I think I'll go and see how she's doing at the hospital. I feel that I need to go and give her some support.' She glanced at him. 'What about you—what are you planning to do?'

'I have to go and talk to the police. I'll probably go to the station to make a statement, but after that I'll come and pick you up from the hospital, if you like. It might be better if you were to come and stay at my place for a few days. That way, you can get your house back to normal before you take Connor home.'

'Are you sure about that?' Alison couldn't think what to do. There was no way she wanted Connor to go back to their house and see the broken window and all the devastation. It would take her some time to clear it all up and get the window fixed.

'I'm sure. As you say, we'll have to find out what Rhea wants to do, but one way or another I'll sort it all out.'

Connor stirred in Allison's arms. He lifted his head a fraction and cast a quick look in Taylor's direction. 'Are we going to your house?' he asked.

'Yes, if that's what your mother wants to do.'

'Say yes, Mummy,' Connor pleaded, looking up at her with tear-filled eyes. 'I want to go there. He looked after me when that bad man was shouting. Can we, Mummy?'

'I expect so. I'll have to see what Rhea wants to do first of all. We can't leave her on her own.'

'Can't she stay at his house with us?' Connor looked at Taylor, his gaze expectant.

Taylor nodded. 'If that's what she wants to do.' He frowned. 'I'll probably have to make a bed up on the couch if we're going to fit everybody in.'

Connor smiled, and it was like a ray of sunshine peeping out from behind the clouds. 'Good,' he said. His eyes were shining with satisfaction, and Allison looked at him and thought how very much he looked like his father at that moment.

She glanced at Taylor, and it struck her that he

was very quiet. He was studying Connor, too, and there was a hint of puzzlement in his steady gaze, as though he was working on a problem and had not yet found the answer. What was he thinking? Was he coming close to discovering the truth?

His expression was bleak, and Allison wasn't at all sure how he would react if he ever managed to work everything out.

CHAPTER EIGHT

RHEA sat patiently in the hospital room while her wrist was being encased in a cast.

'We'll take another X-ray just as soon as we've done this,' the nurse said, 'just to make sure that everything's in the right place. You'll need to let us know if you have any tingling in your fingers, or if you think there's anything untoward going on.'

'I'll do that. Thanks,' Rhea murmured. She glanced at Allison. 'Do you have any idea how long I'll need to wear this cast? It's going to make life difficult for me, but at least it's my left hand, so I should be able to go on doing my work somehow.'

'It might be a few weeks, I'm afraid.' Allison frowned. 'I had a look at the X-ray, and you've broken the scaphoid bone, as Taylor suggested.

It's the small bone at the base of the thumb, but there's a good blood supply there, so it should heal without any problems. If you had broken the middle part it might have been more troublesome.'

'That's something, anyway. It could have been much worse, I guess.' Rhea gave a faint shiver. 'I tried to calm Steve down as best I could, but my nerves were beginning to get the better of me. I was so relieved when Taylor managed to talk his way in. And now that Nick's come to meet me and give me a ride home, I feel so much better.'

She cast a swift glance over to where Nick was sitting with Connor at the other side of the room, and he returned her gaze with a smile. Connor was playing with building blocks that the nurse had been thoughtful enough to provide, and Nick was showing him how to make an intricate construction.

'I felt so angry that Steve could imagine I would let him rule my life like that,' Rhea said. She was still pale and shocked, but something of her old self came to the fore as her annoyance at the situation took over.

'I've decided that I'm through with moving

from place to place. I'm going to stay put from now on.' She gave a weak smile. 'Mind you, I can say that now that I know the police have him in custody. I doubt they'll let him out on bail.'

Allison gave her friend's uninjured hand a gentle squeeze. 'I'm glad that it turned out well enough in the end,' she murmured.

'You won't have to go through anything like that again,' Nick said, coming in on the conversation and sending Rhea a steady look. 'I won't let anything happen to you. As it is, I feel bad about not being there for you when you needed me. From now on I'm going to make sure that you're not on your own.'

Rhea's mouth curved at the corners. 'You're not going to let me forget that I should have waited for you, are you?'

'No, I'm not.' Nick turned back to the building blocks and Connor. 'You've nearly finished that castle. You could put a door in there to finish it off, if you like.'

Connor nodded, and yawned.

'I ought to think about getting him home,' Allison said, and then glanced at Rhea. 'Have you made up your mind what you want to do about staying at Taylor's place?'

'Yes, I have. I've decided to go back to my house after all and face up to my demons,' Rhea answered. 'I don't see why I should let Steve drive me away, any more.'

Allison frowned. 'Are you sure that you feel up to it?'

Rhea nodded, and Nick cut in quickly, 'I'll see to it that Rhea is looked after. She won't be on her own.'

Allison's eyes widened a little at that, but she wasn't about to make any comment in case she disturbed something precious in the making.

'OK, that's good to hear,' she murmured. Was that how the land lay? The two of them had kept things very quiet, hadn't they? Was her brother finally coming around to finding himself a girlfriend? It was a good feeling, knowing that two of the most important people in her life were possibly seizing a chance of happiness at last.

She left them together a short time later, and went to meet up with Taylor at the nurses' station. If only life could be as simple as far as he was concerned.

'Are we going home now?' Connor asked as they headed for the lifts and the car park.

She nodded. 'Taylor says he's going to take us back to his apartment.'

Connor's eyes widened. 'What's an apartment? Hasn't he got a house? Can't he come back to ours?'

Allison hesitated. What was she to tell him? The house was a mess and, apart from calling someone in to board up the broken window, she hadn't had a chance to sort it out.

'My apartment is like a house, but it's in the City and if we stay there it means we won't have far to go if we want to see something of London tomorrow,' Taylor cut in quickly. 'I thought you might like to spend some time going out, doing fun things,' he added.

He glanced at Allison, a question in his eyes. 'Neither of us has to work, and it might be an idea to do something special after all this.'

She realised that he wanted to take Connor's mind off what had happened, and she was perfectly ready to go along with that. In fact, she wanted to hug him for thinking of it.

Instead, she nodded, giving him an uncertain look. 'I think that would be a good idea, if you think you're up to it.' How would he cope, having a four-year-old in tow?

He must have read the question in her eyes, because he said softly, 'I can at least try. He's been through quite an ordeal, and I think some distraction is in order.'

Stepping through the main doors of the hospital and out into the main thoroughfare, Allison looked at Connor. 'Where would you like to go tomorrow?' she asked.

'Can we go and see where the Queen lives?' he asked. 'Rhea was going to take us but she didn't have time.' He frowned. 'And we could go to the farm,' he went on a moment later, gathering momentum. 'I want to sit on the tractors, and see the animals, and play on the swings.' He glanced at Taylor. 'You promised.'

Taylor was laughing by now. 'There won't be much time for anything else, will there, if we do all that? Do you think we might have time to sit and eat?'

Connor nodded vigorously. 'Oh, yes. We can have burger and chips and ice cream and milk-shake. I like that.'

'Well, I think that's tomorrow sorted out,' Taylor murmured. 'I've no idea what we might do for the rest of the week.' By now they had arrived at the car park, and he showed them to his vehicle.

Connor frowned. 'We could go swimming, and to the park, and…' He paused, thinking it through.

'I think I get the picture,' Taylor said, smiling. 'You'll never be short of ideas, will you?'

Connor shook his head, but his mind was busy, planning out the itinerary. 'Are we going on a bus?' he asked. 'I've never been on a bus before.'

'We'll see,' Allison said, helping him into the car. 'Let's just get today over with first, shall we?' She saw that Taylor had a booster seat fitted in the back of the car, and guessed that he was used to transporting his nephews around.

When they arrived at the apartment just a little while later, though, she started to worry all over again. Taylor's place was so beautiful, pristine and luxurious, and the thought of letting a four-year-old loose in here was beginning to weigh heavily on her mind.

'Go on up to the living room,' Taylor said. 'I just want to gather up my post from the hall table, and I'll be with you in a moment.'

Allison showed Connor upstairs. 'You have to be careful not to break anything in here,' she told him as she pushed open the door to the living room, 'and we don't want to find any dirty fingermarks appearing anywhere, so no touching the glass with sticky fingers. Do you understand?'

Connor nodded, wide-eyed, as he looked around. 'Do you mean like this glass?' he asked, exploring the edge of the coffee-table with the tips of his fingers.

Allison groaned inwardly. 'That's exactly what I mean,' she said. 'And the cooker and the mirrors, and all the shelves.' She looked at the beautiful, delicately fashioned ornaments that had been so carefully arranged, and gave a little shudder. 'Especially the shelves,' she added.

Taylor came in and must have heard what they

were saying. 'I don't want you to worry about any of that,' he said. 'You must use this place as if it was your own.'

Allison winced. That was easy enough for him to say. What did he know about four-year-old boys and the kind of destruction they were capable of? 'Have your sister's children stayed here before now?' she asked.

He shook his head. 'Not for more than an hour or so. I haven't had the place all that long, and Claire has only popped in on the odd occasion while she's been in the area.'

He looked around, a frown indenting his brow. 'Perhaps I'll just move one or two of the pieces out of harm's way.' Allison watched as he gathered up all of the ceramics and breakable items that were within reach of small hands and moved them to places of safety within various cupboards. Perhaps he wasn't as confident about this idea as he had led her to believe.

He glanced at Connor. 'There's a box of toys in a corner near the dining table,' he said, taking the child by the hand and showing him where to find it. 'Adam and Josh stop by sometimes with their mother, and they like to have something to keep them occupied.' He sent Allison a crooked grin. 'I find it's better for me if they have something to keep them busy,' he said with a wry smile.

Connor sat down and rummaged through the box. 'Wow!' he exclaimed. 'There's a train set.' He showed Allison what he had found. 'You wind it up with this key, see?' A minute or so later, he was making chug-chugging noises and copying the warning note that a train might make when it approaches a station.

'He seems to be happy enough for the time being,' Taylor murmured, taking Allison to one side. 'I'd better organise the sleeping arrangements. There's a pull-out guest bed that fits under the one in the second bedroom. I'll set that up in the dressing-room for Connor, if that's all right with you?'

'That would be great. Thank you.' She looked up at him. 'I'm really grateful to you for doing all this. I don't think I could have coped with going back to the house just yet. I'm not certain why, but everything seemed to overwhelm me for a while. It was the thought that someone had been there and acted with such hatred. Knowing that it was Steve doesn't make it any less upsetting.'

'I know.' His gaze was sympathetic. 'It must have come as a shock to you, and you might need to take a few days to get over it. Think of this is a breathing space.'

'I will. Thanks.'

Over the next hour or so he made them both feel as though they belonged there, and gradually the horrors of the day and evening began to fade away. He cooked a meal, a surprisingly appetising concoction of vegetables and shepherd's pie that even Connor tucked into without a murmur.

He polished off his fruit salad dessert, and told Taylor, 'This is my very favourite. Well, 'cept for chocolate pudding.' Then he yawned widely, and tried to pretend that he was still fully alert and ready for action.

'It's very late,' Allison told him, 'and way past your bedtime. We should start thinking about getting you settled down for bed.' She helped the little boy down from his chair, and led him to the bathroom to clean up.

Taylor produced some pyjamas that he kept to one side for his sister's children. 'They've never actually had occasion to use them,' he said, 'but Claire wanted me keep them here just in case. They might be a bit big for him, but you can always turn back the sleeves. There are some trousers and a few T-shirts and socks Connor could use, as well.' He made a wry face. 'You know how ditzy Claire is… even she knows there's always the chance she might have some crisis to deal with, and having the boys stay here is one option that might come in handy.'

Soon Connor was snuggled into the guest bed, tucked under a warm duvet. He looked around the strange room and started to whimper. 'I want my room,' he said. 'Why can't I have my room?'

'You can, in a little while,' Allison murmured, stroking his hair. 'It's all right. I'm here with you, and I'll stay until you fall asleep.' She dropped a gentle kiss on his cheek.

It wasn't long before his eyelids started to

droop, and within minutes he was asleep. Allison crept silently out of the room.

Taylor was making coffee in the kitchen when she went back upstairs. 'Has he settled down?' he asked, and she nodded. 'That's good,' he said softly. 'I wondered if being in a strange place would upset him.'

'He's very tired. It's been a long day for him.'

She helped him to set a tray with coffee-cups and cream, and he carried it into the living room, placing it on the low table.

'Do you think Rhea will be all right back at her place?' he asked, coming to sit beside her on the corner sofa. 'I offered to find room for her here, but she turned me down. She said something about Nick coming to keep an eye on her.' He lifted a brow at that.

'Yes, that surprised me, too.' Her mouth twisted wryly. 'I hope she'll be OK, and I felt bad about leaving her, but she was positive that was what she wanted. If anyone can help her through this, Nick is the one to do it. They've always been good friends…it's just that I didn't realise there was anything more to it. Nick has always said that he didn't want to get involved with anyone in any kind of committed relationship.'

'Was that because of the way things were at home?'

She nodded, taking a sip of her coffee. 'It was very difficult, living in a place where there were constant arguments, and I think that was all because my parents were never really suited to one another. They were opposites, and I can't think how they ever came to get together in the first place. There was constant friction between them. My father was a wanderer, always looking beyond the horizon, wanting to take on some new challenge, and my mother was a home bird, needing to be close to her family. She couldn't understand why he wasn't ready to settle in one place.' She frowned. 'I suppose I'm the same as she was.'

She glanced at him, her green eyes cloudy. 'I'm not like you, ready to go off at any time in search of new challenges. I like to know where my roots are, and I need to be close to the people I love.'

'Yet you've been ambitious in your own way, haven't you?' Taylor drank some of his coffee and then put down his cup. 'You could have settled for being a GP, with working hours that might fit in around your family responsibilities, but instead of that you went ahead with your plans to work in A and E. That can't have been an easy choice. It's a difficult job at the best of times.'

'That's true enough. I just felt that I could make more of a difference in emergency situations. I don't think I would need to travel the country to find a place to do that, though. Perhaps my ambitions aren't as great as yours and, besides, I don't want to uproot Connor any more than I have to.'

'It must have been difficult for you, looking after him these past few years and taking on the role of both mother and father. You haven't had any help from your own father, have you?'

She shook her head. 'No, not a great deal. He's always working away somewhere. Connor knows that he has a grandad, and he sees him from time to time, but there isn't an awful lot of contact.'

'That must be hard for you, especially with your mother not being around any more. It must make you feel very isolated.'

'Yes, it does, sometimes.' It seemed odd to

her that he should understand. He was a confident man, always in control, and he had never
appeared to need anybody.

'Do you feel much the same way that Nick
does about getting involved with someone? Is
that why you haven't let a man into your life?
You must have thought about getting together
with Connor's father?'

She hesitated, hovering on the brink of telling
him the truth. 'Yes, I think I do feel much the same
way. I'm always afraid that things won't work out,
and I can't put that uncertainty on Connor. Above
all, I need to be sure that he has security.'

He moved closer to her, sliding an arm around
her and drawing her to him. 'Surely, he'll get
that just by being with you? Aren't you the one
certain thing in his life?'

She loved the familiarity of having him hold
her close. 'I hope so. I don't know.' She looked
up at him, her gaze troubled. 'When things
happen as they did this afternoon, I feel as
though my whole world is crumbling around
me. I know I shouldn't feel that way, because
Rhea was the one who was hurt, and she was the

one who had to go through all the trauma, but it just brought it all home to me, how vulnerable we are. Rhea's so capable, in her own way, but I don't know if I can live up to her example. I don't know if I'm strong enough to take care of Connor on my own. I should have been there for him. I feel that I let him down and I owe him so much more than that.'

'Rhea has always been adept at meeting things head on but, then again, she has always had her family behind her. She knows that her parents are there if she needs them. That's her safety net.' He frowned. 'You're just as capable as she is, and though you may feel otherwise, you're not alone. You have friends, a brother who loves you… And you have me… I want you to know that I'm here to help you through your troubles.'

Allison knew that he was sincere in what he was saying, but that was now, in the heat of the moment. How long would he be staying around to help out? The question reverberated through her mind, but there was no answer forthcoming.

Perhaps he sensed her turmoil, because he gave her a searching look and then bent his head to hers, and she was absorbed into another world as he drew her to him. He kissed her, gently brushing his lips over hers and testing the softness of her mouth, and as the kiss deepened, she realised that this was what she wanted, more than anything. Her whole body tingled in response, and every sensible thought flew out of her mind in that instant.

She returned the kiss, running her fingers over his strong arms in tender exploration, loving the feel of him. She needed this closeness, this wonderful moment when he wrapped his arms around her and crushed her to him.

His hand stroked the length of her spine, tracing the curve of her hip and lingering on the smooth expanse of her thigh, and she treasured that moment, delighting in that warm caress.

Taylor was everything she wanted. His kisses swept her along in a torrent of desire, of desperate, urgent need, and it seemed as though he must feel the same way, too, because she felt his heart thundering against hers, an echo of her own.

'Allison,' he murmured, trailing kisses over her cheek and dipping lower, letting his lips glide along the line of her throat. 'Do you know what you do to me? You make me lose all control. What am I to do? I'm hungry for you. I want you.'

She wanted him, too, but she had made this mistake before, and the consequences had been far greater than she ever could have imagined. His need was temporary, wasn't it, a fleeting passion that would surely dissolve in the light of day? When had he ever said that he wanted anything more than a few brief moments of bliss?

She tried to clear the fog that was clouding her brain, and already she had begun to ease back from him. Taylor looked down at her. 'Allison?'

She opened her mouth to answer him, but then a soft padding sound intruded on her thoughts. Taylor must have heard it, too, because he became very still for a moment, and then started to draw back from her. Then the padding became a clatter as though someone was clutching at a doorhandle.

By the time the stairs door opened, they had both sprung back from one another.

'Mummy, you wasn't there.' Connor stood in

the doorway, recrimination written on his pink mouth. 'Where was you?'

'I'm here, sweetheart.' Allison scrambled to get herself together. 'I wasn't far away.'

'There was a bad man in my room. He was shouting at me.'

She went over to him and gathered him up in her arms. 'It was just a dream, angel. The bad man has gone away, I promise.'

'Do you?'

'Yes, I do.'

Sleepily, he laid his head on her shoulder. 'Can I have some milk? I don't want to go back to bed.'

'I'll get it,' Taylor said. He sent Allison a quick, searching glance, and his mouth made a crooked slant in recognition that their few moments of togetherness were over. Then he looked back at Connor. 'How about some hot chocolate?'

Connor nodded, putting his thumb into his mouth. He watched Taylor walk to the kitchen and take a pan from the cupboard, ready to heat the milk.

Allison sat with him for a while, helping him

with his cup when Taylor returned. When he had finished drinking from it, she put the cup to one side and held him while he settled back to sleep. 'I'll take him back to bed,' she murmured, glancing at Taylor some time later.

'Do you want me to carry him for you?'

She shook her head. 'I'll manage, thanks.' She hesitated. 'I'll stay with him for a while, to make sure that he's all right, and then I think I'll go to bed myself. We've all had a difficult day.'

'All right.' His grey eyes were dark, smokily unreadable. 'I'll see you in the morning.'

'Yes.'

CHAPTER NINE

THE next day, they were all up and about early, getting ready for their trip out. Allison was glad to be going away from the apartment. The thought of what her impish son might get up to in the confines of the flat was disturbing her more than a little and Taylor's occasional concerned glances when it looked as though her child might bump into things only served to ratchet up her tension.

Taylor had arranged for them to travel by bus to visit a couple of London landmarks, but when they approached the bus stop, Connor looked as though he was taken aback.

'Is that a proper bus?' he asked. 'Something's wrong with it.'

'It's a special bus,' Taylor said, laughing. 'It's an open-top one. It means you can go up the stairs and sit at the top of the bus in the open air.

I thought you would like it, and that it might be exciting for you to do that.'

Connor looked dubious at first, but Allison persuaded him to try it out, and soon he was giggling at the way the breeze riffled through his hair, and he was holding on to the bar in front of him, pretending to drive.

A short time later they arrived at The London Eye, the huge wheel close to the River Thames. They went aboard, and as it began to move slowly through its circular arc, Taylor pointed out for Connor some of the tall buildings in the distance.

'That's Westminster Bridge nearby, going over the River Thames, and just on the other side of the water you can see the Houses of Parliament and Big Ben.'

'Who's Big Ben?'

'It's not a who,' Allison said. 'It's a building…a clock tower. See? It's very tall, isn't it?'

Connor nodded. He turned around to look in the opposite direction, and surveyed the view.

'That big building next to Tower Bridge, way in the distance across the water, is the Tower of

London,' Taylor murmured. 'Can you see the four turrets sticking up in the air?'

Connor nodded.

'And a bit to one side, the curved blue glass building that stands out from all the others is the Swiss Re building. It looks a bit like the shape of a pickle, so some people call it the Gherkin. It's one of the tallest buildings in the City.'

Connor looked around him, but seemed to be unimpressed by the vision of the London land-scape. If Taylor was disappointed by his lack of interest, he didn't make any comment, but simply stood and absorbed the view for himself.

Connor, in the meantime, was more caught up in examining the inside of the glass capsule and in running his hands along the metal rail.

'Look down there, at the water,' he said to Allison. 'There's lots of boats. Will they bang into each other?'

'I shouldn't think so,' Allison murmured. 'Let's hope they all look where they're going.'

The journey came to an end just a few minutes later, and Allison held Connor's hand as they disembarked. Taylor laid a hand on the small of her back as they disembarked, steering her out into the street.

She liked the warm, gentle touch of his hand on her spine, but she was trying her best not to get too used to it. Today was a jewel in the crown, but tomorrow the crown might be snatched away. Taylor already had a job in mind that would eventually take him away from them, and even if by chance he were to stay around and want to be with them, how could she know that he wouldn't tire of being slowed down by the demands of a small child? So far, he was bearing up pretty well, but how long would it last?

'Where are we going now?' Connor asked, as they boarded another open-top bus.

'You wanted to see Buckingham Palace, didn't you?' Taylor raised an eyebrow. 'I thought we'd take a quick look there, before we make tracks for the farm.'

'OK.' Connor was happy enough to go along with that. 'Will we be able to go inside?'

'Not today,' Allison told him. 'It isn't open for visitors right now, so we'll just stay outside and watch the soldiers parade in their red uniforms for a little while.'

Connor's face lit up as he saw the guards assemble in front of the Palace just a short while later. He watched them march in time to the music from the band, and he joined in, marching on the spot. Allison began to smile, and when she looked up at Taylor, she saw that he, too, was trying to suppress a grin. They exchanged glances, and he moved closer to her, sliding an arm around her shoulders.

'I think he's recovering well from yesterday's upset, don't you?'

'I do.' His touch was casual, but familiar and enfolding at the same time. It made her feel good inside.

'Does the Queen live in there?' Connor waved a hand towards the Palace.

'Yes, sometimes. She has other places where she can stay, but if the flag is flying, it means she's at home.' Taylor glanced at him. 'It's flying today, see?'

Connor nodded. 'Why can't we see her and say hello?'

'Well, she's a very busy lady. She has work to do.'

'Oh.' Connor thought about that. 'There must be a lot of rooms in there.' He seemed awed by the size of the building. 'How many bedrooms does she have?'

'About fifty, I think.'

'Fifty?' Connor's eyes widened, and he looked at Allison for confirmation. 'Does she sleep in a different one every night?'

'Well, I suppose she could, if she wanted to,' Allison murmured, her mouth curving, 'but I think she probably just keeps one for herself. The others are for her family, or for important people who go to stay at the Palace sometimes.'

'Oh,' Connor said. He looked at Taylor. 'Can we go to the farm now?'

Taylor looked back at him. 'Is that it, then? Have you had enough here? Don't you like looking at the Palace?'

'Yes, I do like it, but I want to go to the farm now.'

Taylor sent Allison an oblique glance. He looked a touch bewildered, and she said with a smile, 'That's what four-year-olds are like. They have the attention span of a gnat.'

He nodded and made a crooked grin. 'Of course, I knew that.'

Allison laughed. 'No, you didn't. You haven't a clue about young children, if the truth were known.'

'I have, too.' He chuckled, his eyes bright with amusement. His gaze ran over her, lingering on the flyaway golden strands of her hair and coming to rest on the fullness of her pink lips. He seemed to be mesmerised for a moment, and then he leaned towards her, and on an impulse he planted a kiss on her startled mouth.

Allison didn't have time to register a coherent response, because Connor said in a puzzled tone, 'What are you doing?'

He was tugging on Taylor's jacket, and looking up at him, a frown in his eyes.

'I…uh…I was kissing your mummy.'
'Why?'

Taylor looked flummoxed for a moment. 'Well…because she looked so pretty, and sweet, and I thought it would be a nice thing to do.'

'Oh.' Connor was still frowning, trying to take on board the complexities of adult behaviour. 'Can we go now?'

Taylor nodded. 'All right.' He glanced at Allison, who was still fizzing inside with exhilaration from the unexpected kiss. 'I guess you're right. I've a lot to learn.' He turned back to Connor. 'All right, we'll head for the farm. Perhaps we should get something to eat once we get there.'

'Not until after he's played on the swings and roundabouts,' Allison put in, coming to her senses at last and sounding a note of caution. 'I don't want him throwing up all over the place.'

Taylor winced. 'Yuck. I'd forgotten that little boys tend to do that.'

They headed for the farm, picking up Taylor's car from the garage and driving out to West London. 'It'll be easier this way,' Taylor said. 'The buses were just something that I thought he might enjoy, but I expect he'll be glad of a car ride by the time we start out for home later on.'

Connor was in his element at the farm. There was an adventure playground where he ran about and used up some of his excess energy, climbing on logs and swinging on old tyres, and it was only after all that activity that he was ready to sit down and eat lunch.

Allison had a cheese salad, while Taylor and Connor tucked into burgers and chips. She was glad to see that Connor ate heartily and seemed to be suffering no after-effects from the day before. It was a good thing that Taylor had suggested this outing. It meant that there had been no time for Connor to dwell on what had happened.

Connor swallowed the last of his milkshake and put his glass down on the table, looking thoughtfully up at Taylor. 'I had a good time today. Can we do this again another day?'

'I expect we could, some time,' Taylor answered cautiously. He speared a chip with his fork.

Connor looked him over, tilting his head on one side as he inspected him from top to toe. 'I like you,' he said. 'Are you my daddy?'

Taylor was eating, but now he spluttered on his food and swallowed hastily. 'Um…' He blinked, and Allison could see that he didn't know what he should say, and neither did she.

Coming out of the blue this way, she had no idea how best to handle the situation.

'I think perhaps it would be best if you were to talk to your mother about that.' Taylor recovered himself well enough and looked at the little boy, his expression serious.

'Yes, but she says Daddy doesn't live with us, but now you do, and anyway, I'd like to have you for my daddy. Can't you be my pretend daddy?'

Taylor put down his knife and fork and gave the child his full attention. 'Is this something that's very important to you?'

Connor nodded solemnly.

'What kind of thing would you want to happen?'

'Well, I like going out places, and I like the toys you have in your house. It was good when you looked after me when the bad man was shouting, 'cos you were kind and you looked after Rhea.' He ran out of steam momentarily and gave Taylor an anxious stare.

'It's something I need to think about,' Taylor said, 'and of course I have to talk to your mother about it a little bit. Is it all right with you if we say that we're friends for now? Good friends?'

Connor gave an awkward little shrug. It wasn't the answer he wanted, but it looked as though Taylor had at least left him something to be going on with.

Taylor glanced at Allison. She was still taken aback by what her son had said, and for now she had absolutely no notion of what was the right thing to say or do.

She handed Connor a napkin so that he could wipe his face and hands. 'Being friends is a great idea,' she said. 'I think we need some time to think about the rest of it.' She paused, letting that sink in. 'Should we go and find the tractors and toy cars for you to ride on? And then we could go and look at the pet corner, if you like.'

'OK.' Connor's mood changed like quicksilver, and he slid down from his chair, ready for action.

Allison knew that it was a get-out on her part, that she was stalling, and Taylor was aware of that, too. He studied her thoughtfully for a while as she gathered up their belongings, and then he held Connor's hand as the boy tugged him in the direction of the activity toys.

'I want a yellow car to ride on if I can,' Connor

told him. 'Mummy says I don't have to wait until Christmas. She might buy me one for my birthday, if I'm really, really good. I can be good, you know. Sometimes I forget, but only a tiny bit.' He looked up at Taylor. 'Do you think that will be all right?'

'I think so, yes,' he answered soberly. 'No one can be good all the time.' He sent the child a questioning gaze. 'When is your birthday, do you know?'

Connor screwed up his face. 'I'm not sure. It isn't now, I know that…but Mummy says it's in three months' time. Is that a long while?'

'It depends on how eager you are to have your car,' Taylor murmured. 'Three months isn't all that long, really. It means your birthday is in September.' He glanced at him. 'You'll be five, then, won't you?'

'Yes, and I won't be in the nursery any more. I'll be in the big school then.'

'Yes, you will.' Taylor was silent after that, and looking at him and seeing his taut expression, Allison was worried about what was going on in his mind.

He didn't say anything about what he was thinking, and for the rest of the afternoon he devoted his attention to Connor, helping him onto the tractors and showing him how to feed the animals with food supplied by the farm.

It was the very quietness of his manner that bothered Allison. He had been very careful in the way he had questioned Connor about his birthday, and he had been thoughtful ever since. Had he taken all that information and worked out the date when her son was conceived?

He drove them home later that day, and even prepared supper for them while she sorted out the grubby T-shirt and sweater Connor had discarded and washed them through at the sink. Then she ran the iron over one or two items that he would need for the next day.

She readied Connor for bed. It had been a long, busy day, and the child was tired, but happy, and hopefully all thoughts of his ordeal with Steve and Rhea had gone from his mind.

She tucked him up in bed and kissed him goodnight, staying with him until he had fallen asleep. Then she went quietly back to the living room where Taylor was clearing away the crockery from the table and loading the dishwasher.

Even in profile, his expression was grim, and she guessed that he must have finally worked things out for himself. Her heart plummeted like a lead weight. He didn't look as though he was at all pleased by what he had discovered. In fact, when he turned his gaze on her, his eyes were glittering with anger.

'He's my child, isn't he?' His tone was filled with accusation.

She lifted her chin. 'Yes, he is.' She watched the look of rage flit across his features.

'So why didn't you tell me?' He glared at her. 'Why did you keep it to yourself for all this time? Why did you let me believe that he was someone else's child?'

Allison stood her ground. She had never seen him this irate before, but she couldn't afford to let the fear of his wrath undermine her. Hadn't she done everything with the best of intentions?

'Why would I tell you? You made it pretty clear five years ago that you didn't want a family, and you don't appear to have changed your opinion at all since then. You went away and hardly gave me a backward glance.'

His jaw clenched. 'I'd say you were the one who walked away, wouldn't you? Where were you the next day? You didn't stay around long enough to even say goodbye.'

'I couldn't bring myself to do that. I was alarmed. I felt that what had happened between us had all come about by chance, and I was ashamed of myself for behaving that way.'

'Well, thanks a lot for that.' His mouth made a bitter line. 'That makes me feel really good about myself, doesn't it? You were alarmed and ashamed. It doesn't say a lot that's good about what we experienced together, does it?'

'I didn't mean it like that. For me, it was something that had never happened before. I'd always thought that the first time would be something special, that I would have been involved in a deep and meaningful relationship, and that I would feel loved and cherished, but it didn't happen that way. It was all a matter of unforeseen circumstances and I didn't know what to think.'

In fact, it *had* been special and somehow

precious, and he had made her feel as though she had been the most important thing in the world to him, but it had occurred to her afterwards that perhaps he would have been like that with anyone. She had been young and confused back then. It wasn't as though he had gone out of his way to romance her before that, and she hadn't wanted to feel that she had been an afterthought, that she had just happened to drop into his lap like a ripe plum.

His gaze raked her from head to toe. 'Was that supposed to make me feel any better? Let me tell you, it didn't. I'd say it had the opposite effect.' His eyes narrowed on her. 'Why didn't you get in touch with me as soon as you knew that you were pregnant? If you really didn't know where I was working, you could have gone to my parents and asked them for my address.'

'What would have been the point? Would you have rushed back to me and given up the chance of being a consultant in order to stay home and change nappies?' She shook her head. 'I don't think so.' She grimaced. 'I didn't believe you would want to know, and even if you had made an effort to do the decent thing, I didn't want to build a relationship based on a one-time lapse. I saw enough of what can happen when things go wrong, by watching my parents live out their mistakes.'

His voice was cold with fury. 'You didn't even give me the chance to decide what to do, one way or the other, did you? How was I supposed to do the right thing, or work out what it was that I felt about having a son, if you didn't tell me in the first place? Who knows whether we might have worked things out between us? For all you know, we could have brought him up together, so that he might be fulfilled as part of a wider family, but all that has gone by the wayside now. The boy is desperate for a father, and you've denied him that ever since he was born.'

She swallowed hard. His words cut her like knives, the more so because she knew that what he was saying was the truth. Had she made the wrong choice, right from the start?

'How could he ever have known the satisfaction of being part of a wider family?' she countered. 'You and my brother were barely on speaking terms. What would that have done for my child's confidence, knowing that the family was ripped apart?'

His mouth tightened. '*Your* child? Let's get this right, shall we? He's *our* child...yours and mine...and it's high time you started to realise that.'

'All right. He's our child...but that doesn't take away the fact that you hurt my brother, his uncle. How do you plan on reconciling that?'

A muscle flicked in his jaw. 'I don't plan on doing anything. All that concerns me right now is that I have a four-year-old son who needs a father, and who is bound to feel that I've let him down by not being there for him throughout his growing years. That's all down to you. It's your fault, because you kept me in the dark, and I don't know how I'm ever going to come to terms with that.'

CHAPTER TEN

ALLISON dropped Connor off at nursery school next day. He was still bubbling over with enthusiasm about his day out at the farm and he was eager to tell his teacher and his friends all about it.

'I'm going to show everybody the toy hen I bought from the farm shop,' he said, clutching Allison's hand as she led him to the door of the classroom. 'They'll like it when they see how it lays eggs.'

'I'm sure they will.' She kissed him goodbye and watched as he went to join a group of friends on the carpet area in the classroom. He was so busy chatting to them that he almost forgot to wave to her…almost, but not quite. He turned and lifted a hand, and she waved back before leaving for work.

She wasn't looking forward to meeting Taylor

again. He had been there with them for breakfast at the apartment, but it had been a quiet
affair and he had spoken mostly to Connor. His
remarks to Allison had been short and to the
point, mostly to do with her plans for dealing
with the break-in at her house.

'I'll go there after work and make a start on
clearing up,' she told him. 'A glazier's coming
to fix the window, and I should be able to make
the place habitable again within a few hours.
Rhea said she would take care of Connor for me
while I do that. Poppy will be with her and the
children can play together.'

He didn't comment any further, and she guessed
he would be relieved once she had moved out of
his apartment. Why else would he be asking?

Perhaps she might even be able to pack up her
things and move back home later on this evening.
That would probably please Taylor. It made her
sad to know that the atmosphere was so spiky
between them, but it was probably inevitable that
things should turn out this way, and, as he said, she
had only herself to blame. It was beyond her at the
moment to know how she could put things right.

Taylor was treating a child for a peanut allergy when she arrived at the hospital. The girl, who was about six years old, had gone into anaphylactic shock after eating a biscuit, and now she was struggling for breath. In the background a monitor was beeping a warning.

It was heart-wrenching to see her lying there, looking so ill, fighting for her life. Taylor was giving her oxygen and had set up an intravenous line ready for treatment fluids to alleviate the symptoms of shock and hypertension.

'I can't intubate her,' he said, looking grim. 'The tissues in her throat have swollen up too much and I might have to resort to doing a cricothyroidotomy. I'm waiting as long as I dare, to see if the medication works to reduce the swelling before I do that.'

'Her blood pressure is very low,' Allison murmured. 'What medication has she had so far? Adrenaline, antihistamine?'

'Yes, both of those.'

'Shall I give her salbutamol to relieve the bronchospasm?'

He nodded. 'Yes, that should help.'

They worked together for the next few minutes, both of them desperate to save the life of this little girl, and for a while their antipathy towards one another was pushed to one side.

'Her blood oxygen level is rising,' the nurse said a short time later.

Taylor nodded and let out a slow breath. 'That's good. I think maybe we're beginning to get her back at last.' He glanced at Allison. 'Would you go and have a word with the parents? They're in the waiting room, and they must be very anxious for news.'

'I will.'

She left him to take care of the child, and spent a few minutes reassuring the girl's mother and father, as he had asked. It was always difficult, talking to parents who were overwrought with anxiety. In this case, she had good news to share, but it reminded her of the time when she had spoken to the mother of the boy who had taken drugs.

That first meeting had been difficult, because her child's life was in the balance, but eventually there had been another heartfelt discussion, when she had been able to tell her that her son was recovering. Those were the occasions that made her job worthwhile.

When she went back to the main body of A and E a while later, Taylor was already working with another patient, and she decided that the best thing she could do was to keep her head down and follow through on her own patient list. Taylor was not in a communicative mood. He had said his piece last night, and there was nothing she could do to change things.

Her brother called in at the hospital later on that afternoon, and came to find Allison at the desk.

'I've just had the report from the auditors, and they say everything is in order,' Nick told her. 'It's a relief, I can tell you.'

'I can imagine. I'm so glad for you.' She smiled at him. 'I don't suppose they ever managed to find out what went wrong before, did they? Did they look into the books from the previous business?'

He nodded. 'I asked them to do that. It bothered me that things went downhill so fast, and that we lost our customer base. They seem to think it was a question of identity theft, carried out by someone we employed in the office on a casual basis. We had checked out his credentials, but it looks as though he was short of money and decided that the client base was easy pickings. Once he realised that he could get away with it, he became greedy.'

Taylor chose that moment to come over to the desk. He placed a file in the tray and reached for another chart. 'I couldn't help hearing what you said just now,' he murmured. 'Does that mean that they've caught the man?'

Nick inclined his head a fraction. 'A couple of years too late but, yes, the police have finally picked him up. Apparently they raided his flat and found a stash of credit card numbers and addresses and all the private details that he had been using.'

'I'm glad. That must be good news for you.'

'Yes, it is. It will go to court, and they stand a good chance of getting a conviction. The bank will freeze his assets, and it means we can finally write to all our ex-customers and explain the situation. They may be able to make out a case to be heard and possibly they could claim compensation if they've been defrauded in some way. In any case, according to the police and the auditors, we're in the clear.'

Taylor gave a curt nod. 'I can see why you're relieved. It must be a weight off your shoulders.' He held the chart aloft. 'I must go. I have to check up on a patient.'

Allison watched him leave. He hadn't even acknowledged her. 'I wonder if you and he will ever be on good terms, as you were before,' she said in a quiet tone to her brother. 'I just don't know what went wrong.'

'I think I do.' Nick made a face. 'I'd have said something to him about it, but this isn't the place to do it. It turns out that his name was on the list of victims that the police gave to us. I think he must have been stung for a good deal of money, and it's fairly obvious that he thought that was down to us. I suppose he managed to sort it out, but what I don't understand is why he never said anything to us about it.'

Allison was shocked by the news. 'He must have known about the identity theft for years, but he kept quiet about it for all this time. He probably believed that it was either you or Ben, or both, who tried to defraud him.' Her mind was racing. 'Perhaps that's why he wouldn't renew your lease. He wouldn't have wanted either himself or his premises to be associated with anything that reeked of dodgy dealings.'

'I think you could be right.' Nick looked around and saw that the paramedics were bringing in more patients. 'Look, I can see that you're busy here. Do you want me to pick up Connor from school? I know that Rhea offered, but I think she could do with a bit of time to get over what happened, so I said I would take the children to the park—if that's all right with you?'

'Yes, that would be great, thanks.' Allison glanced at him. 'Are you sure that it's all right? Have you finished early for the day?'

He nodded. 'I've left Ben in charge. He's all right about it, because he knows that I want to help Rhea out over the next day or so. You could collect Connor from her house later on, when you've done what you have to do at the house, if you like, or I can bring him over to you.'

'Thanks…whatever you think is best. I'm not sure how long it will take.'

'That's OK. Take as long as you need. I'll be there to keep an eye on things and you can always ring me if there's a problem.'

He left just a few minutes after that, and Allison wrote up her notes on her last patient. Her shift was due to end in half an hour or so, but as she was preparing to hand over to the registrar, a call came in about a major traffic accident.

Taylor was getting ready to go out with the fast-response car, and she said quickly, 'Do you want me to come with you?'

'No, I'll take Greg.'

He didn't say any more, and it was like a slap in the face. She felt as if he was pushing her away, as though he didn't want anything to do with her, and that hurt. It hurt a lot.

There wasn't anything she could do about it, though, and she cleared up all the loose ends at work and made her way to her house.

The police had finished checking it over, and now all that was left for her was to sweep up all the smashed bits and pieces of her belongings and bag them up, ready to be taken to the tip. The glazier came to fix the window, and having someone there with her while she worked was a comfort. The last time she had been there she had recoiled in shock.

When the glazier left, she switched on the radio so that she would have the illusion that she was not alone. It was important to her that she make things as normal as possible for Connor's return, and with that in mind she cleaned and vacuumed and set out a new set of crockery in the kitchen so that it didn't look so bare. In her lunch-break, she had managed to find another teddy-bear mug, not quite the same as the one that had been broken but one that she hoped he would like.

A local news bulletin was being read out on the radio, and some of what was being said caught her attention. 'Traffic accident on the motorway earlier today… Another collision as a lorry careered into the path of rescue workers… Several people injured.'

Allison froze. How could it be possible? They were talking about the accident that Taylor was attending. Was he in danger? What was happening out there? Was Greg all right?

She tried to calm herself down. Surely they would know something at the hospital, if their own colleagues were involved? At least she could ring up and find out, couldn't she?

A minute or two later she spoke to the specialist nurse in A and E. 'We're not sure,' Sarah told her. 'I've been trying to find out what's going on, but all I've been told is that a lorry careered into a response vehicle on the hard shoulder. They say it was a car that was hit, and that's why we're all worried. Apparently the lorry driver was distracted by something or other and swerved to the side of the road.'

'Thanks, Sarah. I think I'll go down there and see for myself what happened. I'll let you know if it's anything at all to do with Taylor or Greg.'

She rang Nick to let him know what was happening, and then she made her way to the site of the accident by car, taking a route to hopefully avoid the worst of the traffic. The motorway was about a mile and a half away from where she lived, and the place where the accident had happened was a notorious black spot. Peak-time traffic had slowed to a crawl because of the emergency vehicles at the scene and when she arrived there she was horrified by the wreckage that met her eyes.

Several cars were crumpled, and a couple of lorries were skewed to one side. The response car was mangled almost beyond recognition.

'Can I do anything to help?' she asked the officer in charge. 'I'm a doctor. I heard about the second collision on the radio.'

'Yes, thanks. We've had several more people injured, mostly fractures, and someone with a chest injury. He was still trapped inside his car until a few minutes ago. I'll take you over there.'

She followed him, hardly daring to ask what was uppermost in her mind. 'Are any of the rescue workers hurt?' she said, struggling to keep her voice on an even note. 'I heard that there were some injured people among them.'

'Yes, we have a couple of men with broken legs, and one with a fractured pelvis. They were working on the other side of the response car when the lorry shunted it sideways.'

'Who are they, do you know?'

By now they had reached the response car. 'One's a paramedic, and the other is a fireman who was bringing over some equipment. I'm not sure about the other man. He may have been a doctor.'

By now Allison's heart was working over-time, pounding heavily against her rib cage. It would be bad enough if Greg was hurt, but she couldn't bear the thought of anything bad hap-pening to Taylor.

They walked around the side of what was left of the response car and Allison scanned the features of the injured people. She recognised the paramedic, being treated for a fractured leg, but the fireman was unknown to her.

Greg was taking care of the fireman. 'I'm so glad that you're all right,' she said. 'When I heard the news bulletin I was afraid you might have been hurt.'

'I'm fine. It's good to see you, Allison.'

She nodded. 'Where's Taylor?'

He grimaced. 'Over there.' He pointed to an area in front of the response car. 'It's nasty. It's an unstable pelvic fracture with massive bleeding. I think they need all the help they can get.'

The officer in charge agreed, and led her to where the injured man was lying on the ground. 'I'll leave you to it, Doctor.'

'Thanks.' Allison felt the blood drain from her face as she approached. The man was being attended by a paramedic and a doctor, both of whom were kneeling at his side, bent over him, and she was desperately afraid for the outcome. She had to keep a tight hold on herself to stop from breaking down.

She tried to see who it was who was injured. 'Taylor,' she said in a cracked voice.

The doctor turned to look at her. 'Allison,' Taylor said, his face showing surprise. 'What are you doing here?'

'Oh…it's you… Thank heaven you're all right.' She gulped in a quick, shaky breath and her mind started to reel. 'I heard news of the collision on the radio and I thought you might be hurt. I was so afraid. I had to come and see for myself what was happening.' She realised that she was babbling, but he didn't seem to be put out by that.

He sent her an odd glance. 'I'm not hurt. I'm OK.' He motioned with his hand, indicating to her to come around the other side of the patient. 'We need some help to get the pelvic sling in place. Could you lend a hand?'

'Yes, of course—that's what I'm here for.' She hoped that she sounded more professional this time.

'Good. See if you can keep this pressure pad in place to stem the bleeding, while we slide the sling around the pelvic area.'

She knelt down beside the man and laid a hand on the pad. The pelvic sling was shaped like a wide belt, and could be fastened in place to prevent movement that would cause any more damage to the pelvic area.

'We'll push bean bags in place around him on the stretcher to maintain his position and keep him even more stable.'

Allison's hand was shaking a little as she helped with the manoeuvres that followed, but she managed to bring herself under control. The patient needed her to be on top form. Taylor was watching her, and he hadn't missed the tremor, she knew, because his glance stayed on her for a moment longer than was strictly necessary and his gaze was thoughtful.

In a while, when Taylor was satisfied that the man was stable enough to be moved, he gave the go-ahead for the transfer to the waiting ambulance.

'I've arranged for a team to be waiting for him at the hospital,' he told the paramedic who would be accompanying him on the journey. 'With luck we've made sure that he has a good chance of recovery, but he'll need to go straight to Radiology and from there to Theatre.'

'OK, I'll see to it that he's monitored on the way.'

Allison went to help out where she was needed. Now that she was reassured that Taylor and Greg weren't harmed in any way, her nerves were beginning to settle down, but she was still edgy and out of sorts. Thinking that Taylor might have been badly hurt had wrung every ounce of composure from her.

'I think we could start making tracks for home now,' Taylor murmured, when all the casualties had been sent on their way to various hospitals in the region.

Allison nodded. She saw that lifting equipment had been brought in to remove the response car, and she said, 'I thought you might have been the one who was injured.'

'And that worried you?'

'Of course it worried me,' she said sharply. 'Though I'd have put it stronger than that. How do you think I felt? I had visions of you lying there with broken bones, or worse. It was scary, really scary.'

He gave a faint smile. 'I'm all right. You can relax now. I'm fine.'

She realised that she had overreacted to his comment, and now her cheeks flushed pink. 'Sorry. It was a bit of a shock, hearing the news like that. I didn't know what to think.' She straightened her shoulders. 'I could give you a lift back to your apartment, if you like.'

'Thanks, that would be good.' He looked at her from under his lashes. 'Perhaps we should go to your house, though. I'll give you a hand with the clearing up.'

'Will you? There isn't a great deal left to do, and I'm sure I can manage, given time. It's more a question of putting the curtain rail back in place. For some reason Steve yanked the curtains down and he must have done it with some force because the fixings have broken off. I'm not quite sure how to go about repairing them.'

'I expect he was in a temper and didn't much think about what he was doing.' His gaze moved over her. 'I'll come with you and see what I can do.'

'Thanks.' She guessed he was still anxious for her to move back to her house as soon as possible, and she wasn't going to put up an argument about that. Connor would be happy to go back to familiar surroundings, and she didn't want to impose on Taylor any more than was necessary.

'I expect Greg will need a lift, too,' she murmured.

'No. He's hitched a ride with one of the para-medics. I asked him what he wanted to do a few minutes ago, and he said he needed to get back home as soon as possible because his wife's mother was staying with them and they were planning an evening out. I think he's already left for home.'

'Oh, I see.' Allison glanced around and realised that what Taylor was saying was true. Most of the rescue personnel had already gone.

They collected up their medical kit and went over to her car. Allison sat behind the wheel for a moment or two, waiting until she had herself together again, and then she drove them to her house.

'It looks pretty much back to normal,' she said. 'It's just a little more sparsely furnished than it was before.'

She parked the car and showed him into the hallway. 'I'll make us a drink and something to eat, if you like,' she murmured. 'You must have gone for ages without any food inside you.'

'Thanks. I'd appreciate that. Just a sandwich would be fine, if that's all right with you.' He followed her into the small kitchen.

Allison was glad of the chance to keep busy. Having Taylor nearby was playing on her nerves and she was strung out all over again at the thought of all the harsh words that had passed between them over the last couple of days. Would he ever forgive her for not telling him about his son?

'I'll see what I can do about the curtain rail in the living room,' he said. 'Do you have a toolbox handy?'

'Yes. I'll get it for you.' She sorted out everything that he might need, and then left him to it, going back to the kitchen to prepare the food.

He was back within a few minutes. 'It's all finished,' he said. 'I've put the curtains back in place for you.'

'Thanks for that.' She looked at him, disturbed by the fact that they were being so cautious around one another, like two strangers meeting up on neutral ground. 'Sit down, won't you?' she said. 'The food's all laid out on the table.'

'I'll just get out of this outfit first.' He removed his outer garments, the medical jacket and over-trousers, placing them on a table in the hallway, and then came back and washed his hands at the sink. He was wearing dark trousers that fitted him to perfection, emphasising his long legs and his flat stomach, and his shirt was a pale blue that reflected the grey-blue of his eyes.

Allison tried not to look at him. It set up all sorts of stirrings of painful emotions within her, just having him there in her house, in her kitchen.

He came and sat down at the table and started to eat, clearly appreciating the fresh sandwiches of cheese, and ham and salad that she had made for them. 'I didn't realise how hungry I was,' he said, glancing across the table at her. His eyes narrowed when he saw that she was empty-handed. 'Aren't you going to eat?'

'I had something earlier.' She couldn't face the thought of food right now. Instead, she sipped at the hot tea and let the liquid warm her through and through. 'I've rung Nick and he's going to bring Connor over here in a while,' she said quietly. 'We can stay here from now on. After all, there's no reason why we should impose on you any longer. I know it must have been difficult for you, having us stay at your place. It was good of you to step in and put us up like that, but I was always worried that we might damage something or spoil all your lovely things.'

'I told you not to worry about that,' he said. 'If I'm not concerned, why should you be?'

'But your place is so beautiful, so…' She hesitated. 'I was going to say untouched, but of course it isn't. It's just so perfect in every way.'

'Perhaps it's time I tried something less than perfect.' He rubbed his fingers on a paper napkin. 'Seeing you here with Connor that night when you made a meal for Rhea and Nick and invited me to join you made me realise how insular my life was becoming. I wondered how I could ever have wanted a quiet, organised existence, free of children, and now I'm beginning to see something of what I've missed all these years. Maybe a little untidiness and home comfort would add something to my life.'

Her eyes widened a fraction. 'Are you saying that now you know that Connor is your child, you want to see what it's like to get involved? Are you thinking of being around for him as a father?' She frowned. 'You've never wanted any of that before.'

'People change.' He looked at her. 'I've changed. I may have something to say about my sister's unruly boys from time to time, but they're part of my family, and I love them dearly. How could I not care for them? They're offshoots of Claire, with all her dizzy, chaotic ways of going on.'

'And Connor? How does he fit in?'

'He's my son. It goes without saying that I want to do my best for him. I would never have turned my back on my child…you were wrong in thinking that I wouldn't want to know.'

'I'm sorry.' She sent him a troubled glance. 'I did what I thought was best at the time. I was confused and anxious, and I wasn't sure how things would turn out.'

'I know that.' His gaze met hers briefly. 'I was angry when you first admitted the truth. I couldn't accept that you had kept it from me for so long, but I think it's time now that we made some decisions about his future. We have to tell him that I'm his father.'

Allison felt a stab of alarm. 'Are you sure that you want to do that?' She saw his brows shoot up in a dark line and she added swiftly, 'What's going to happen when you go away?

How is he going to feel when you disappear from his life?'

'What do you mean? Why should I disappear?'

She frowned. 'You'll be in Hampshire, taking on the role of consultant in the hospital there, won't you? I know that isn't too far away, but it isn't likely that you'll be able to be with him every day, and how is he going to react then? He'll just about be used to the idea of having you around and then you'll be gone. He probably won't see any more of you than he does of his grandad, and he'll be bewildered. He won't understand.'

Taylor opened his mouth to answer, but just then the doorbell rang, and Allison stood up. 'I expect that will be Nick, bringing Connor back home.'

She went to the door and let both of them in. Connor wrapped his arms around her legs and she gave him a hug in greeting. Then he scooted into the living room in search of his toys.

'Thanks for looking after him and bringing him back to me,' she told her brother. 'There's some tea in the pot. Do you have time to stay?'

'Only for a quick cup,' he said. 'I need to get back to Rhea.'

He went to say hello to Taylor, who by now was in the living room, by the dining corner, watching Connor enthusiastically rummage through his toy box.

'We've been playing at Poppy's house,' Connor said, 'but she don't have any toy soldiers. I like playing with soldiers.' He delved deeper in the box until he found what he was looking for. 'This one's wearing his special boots, see?' he said, holding his toy aloft. 'He's my bestest.'

Allison brought a tray of tea into the room and set it down on the dining table. Taylor and Nick were faintly guarded around one another to begin with, but Nick said quietly, 'I realised why you were anxious to move us out of your factory unit as soon as I saw your name on the list of people who had been cheated. I'm sorry about that.' He hesitated for a second or two. 'I don't understand why you didn't say what was on your mind at the time.'

Taylor gave a slight shrug. 'I think I was worried about involving Allison in any kind of trouble. I knew that she had invested some of her own money in the business.'

Allison darted a glance at him. Had he been trying to protect her?

She could see that Nick was anxious to clear up the matter once and for all. 'Did you think that your name might be linked with our company,' he asked, 'if it turned out that Ben and I were the ones behind the trouble?'

'Yes, basically. I thought it best to remove any chance of that happening.' Taylor made a wry face. 'I should have made more enquiries at the time, but I guessed it would be hard to get to the root of the matter and, besides, I thought I was the only victim. I believed that if it had happened to me, it might happen to others, but I didn't know that was the case until later.'

'I wish you had said something, we would have investigated. But I can see how you wouldn't have wanted Allison to be tarred with the same brush. I hope we can put all this behind us now?'

'Yes, of course.'

Nick gave a quick smile. 'I'm glad about that.' He finished off his tea and then said, 'I have to go. Rhea will be waiting for me.'

'OK, I'll see you out.' Allison spoke with him

for a few minutes, and then watched her brother drive away. She was glad that he had sorted out his problems with Taylor. If only she could do the same. She walked back into the living room.

Taylor and Connor were talking to one another, and the little boy's expression was so earnest that for a moment or two she caught her breath, wondering if Taylor had decided to tell him the truth about his parentage without waiting for her agreement.

He must have seen the worried look on her face because he said carefully, 'I've just been asking Connor how he would feel if I were to stay around for a long time. He said he would like that.'

Allison passed her tongue over dry lips. 'But how can that happen if you're planning on going to Hampshire?'

'I'm not.'

She stared at him. 'But you said you had the offer of a job there.'

'I didn't say that I was going to take it. I still have several months to go with the job here in London, and I've been asked if I would consider staying on when that contract finishes. I've been waiting to see how you felt about that before I made the decision.'

She stared at him. 'You were going to ask me how I feel about it?'

'That's right.'

'But…'

'Perhaps we should go and sit down and talk this through?'

'Yes, I think perhaps we should.' Allison glanced at Connor, but he was happily engrossed in playing with his toys once more.

She went over to the settee at the far corner of the room and sat down. For some reason, Taylor's surprise announcement had left her feeling very odd. Her limbs were weak, and her nervous system had suddenly gone on the defensive. What was on his mind? Was he thinking of staying around for Connor's sake? Did she even figure in his reasoning?

Taylor came and sat beside her. He kept his voice low. 'I know that you're wary about talking to me about any of this, and I can understand how you must feel. I was angry with you yesterday, but that was because all of this came as a shock to me and I didn't know what had been going on in your head. I think I realise now why you acted as you did, and I can't really blame you for that. You did what you thought was for the best. You did it for Connor.'

She glanced over to where Connor was playing. He was sitting on the rug in a corner of the room that was partly hidden by an alcove, but she could just make out his small figure.

'I wanted him to have a father, but I didn't think that would come about. I was afraid your career would come before everything, just as my father's did.'

He shook his head. 'Allison, I'm never going to be the same as your father when it comes to my family. If I'd known that you were carrying my child, I would have come back to you. I'd have tried to persuade you to come with me while I worked my way up the career ladder, but in the end the decision would have been yours.'

He slid an arm around her, tugging her close. 'Don't you know how I feel about you? Don't you know that I've always longed to have you by my side?'

Her pulse quickened. 'Have you?' She sent him a doubtful look. Surely what he was saying was too wonderful to be true? Was he just saying it because he wanted to do the right thing by Connor?

He nodded. 'I mean it. I've always known that you were special, but I couldn't tell you. When we were younger, when you were just a teenager, it didn't seem fair to tie you down when you were just starting out on your own path. And later I didn't know how you felt about me. You said what happened between us the night that Connor was conceived was a mistake, something that you regretted, and yet for me it was breathtaking, a time when I realised that you were the one woman I wanted to share my life with.'

Her heart seemed to turn over. 'You didn't say anything...'

His mouth slanted wryly. 'Your note told me what you thought, that you had acted out of character and that we would go our separate ways, and that's how it turned out, didn't it? I went to work as a specialist registrar, and you went to take up your house officer post at a different hospital. I thought we might get in touch, but I didn't know where you were until I saw your name on the staff list at King's Bridge. That's when I made up my mind to accept the year-long contract they were offering me.'

She swallowed hard. Her heart was thumping, causing a pulse to hammer wildly in her throat, but above all a soaring sense of joy was beginning to fill her whole being. 'You came there to be with me?'

'Yes, I did.' He smiled into her eyes. 'I love you, Allison. I've loved you for as long as I can remember. You've always been the one woman who could make me whole, but I didn't know whether you would ever feel the same way about me. It was only when I saw how worried you were earlier this evening, when you thought I might be hurt, that I realised you might care for me more than just a little.'

He had said he loved her. Inside, her heart swelled up. She said softly, 'I didn't know that was how you felt. How could I know? I love you, and I wanted you to love me in return, but I thought it was an impossible dream. I've longed to have you say those things to me, but I was afraid that you couldn't find it in you to love me, or our child.'

A low groan rumbled in his throat. He wrapped his arms around her and kissed her, long and hard, as though he would wipe all doubt from her mind. Their bodies met in sweet unison as he crushed her to him, and she tentatively reached up and touched his face, tracing the contours with the tips of her fingers so that she could keep the image in her heart for ever.

He trailed tender kisses over her cheek. 'I think, deep down, I began to sense that he was my son some time ago. I felt this strange affinity with him, as though there was a hidden bond between us. I had an overpowering need to get to know him better, and at the same time I was trying to work out how I could show you that you had nothing to fear from being with me. I'll always love you and take care of you.'

He claimed her lips once more and she clung

to him, elated by his passionate, loving caresses, by the way he made her know that she was everything in the world that he wanted. His hands stroked her cheek, his thumbs tenderly brushing the softness of her skin, and as she absorbed the sweet promise of his gentle embrace, she suddenly became aware of the light patter of feet and a gentle tugging at her skirt.

Taylor must have noticed that something was amiss, too, because he turned his head a fraction to look at the small boy who was staring up at them.

'What are you doing?' Connor asked.

Taylor began to smile. 'I think we've been here before,' he murmured.

'You'd better get used to it,' Allison said, with a soft chuckle. 'This is how four-year-olds are.'

Connor's stare was unblinking, and Taylor said gently, 'I'm kissing your mummy.'

'You did that before.'

'Yes, well...I like kissing your mummy. I think I might do it lots of times.'

Connor screwed up his nose. 'Why?'

'Because I love her very much, and because

she's just told me that I'm your real daddy. I think we might want to get married and live together and be a proper family, you, your mummy and I. What do you think about that?'

'You're my real daddy? My real, real daddy?' Connor's eyes grew wide, letting his astonishment shine through, but all the while his mouth was breaking into a huge smile.

'I'm your real daddy. I didn't know about you because I was working a long way away, but now that I know you're my little boy I'll stay here with you and your mother for always.'

'For always?' Connor's eyes were still wide. 'Would we all live together here?'

Taylor thought about it. 'I don't know about that. We'd probably need to find a bigger house, one that has a lot more space in the garden so that there will be room for you to ride your car when you get it.'

Allison dug him lightly in the ribs. 'Don't start promising him the world, because you'll have to live up to it.'

Taylor nodded. 'I know that. I mean everything that I'm saying.' He reached down to pick up the little boy and then he placed him between them on the settee. He put an arm around Allison and the other he wrapped around Connor's middle. Allison snuggled into Taylor's shoulder and added her hand to cradle her son.

'So this is how it goes,' Taylor murmured. 'One, your mother and I get married.' He glanced at Allison for confirmation.

'Oh, yes,' she said. 'That's definitely number one.'

'Two, we find a big, beautiful house.'

'With a garden for my car…and a puppy,' Connor said. 'We can have a puppy if we have a garden, can't we?'

'Um…a garden, yes,' Allison said. 'A puppy… maybe. That's going to be one of the first things we get together to think about as a family.' She looked at Taylor. 'What's number three?'

'I know that one,' Connor said. 'We all live happily ever after.'

They all started to laugh at that, and over the top of Connor's head Taylor turned to Allison and stole a soft kiss. She knew that it was going to be the first of many.

MEDICAL™

Large Print

Titles for the next six months...

April

THE ITALIAN COUNT'S BABY	Amy Andrews
THE NURSE HE'S BEEN WAITING FOR	Meredith Webber
HIS LONG-AWAITED BRIDE	Jessica Matthews
A WOMAN TO BELONG TO	Fiona Lowe
WEDDING AT PELICAN BEACH	Emily Forbes
DR CAMPBELL'S SECRET SON	Anne Fraser

May

THE MAGIC OF CHRISTMAS	Sarah Morgan
THEIR LOST-AND-FOUND FAMILY	Marion Lennox
CHRISTMAS BRIDE-TO-BE	Alison Roberts
HIS CHRISTMAS PROPOSAL	Lucy Clark
BABY: FOUND AT CHRISTMAS	Laura Iding
THE DOCTOR'S PREGNANCY BOMBSHELL	Janice Lynn

June

CHRISTMAS EVE BABY	Caroline Anderson
LONG-LOST SON: BRAND-NEW FAMILY	Lilian Darcy
THEIR LITTLE CHRISTMAS MIRACLE	Jennifer Taylor
TWINS FOR A CHRISTMAS BRIDE	Josie Metcalfe
THE DOCTOR'S VERY SPECIAL CHRISTMAS	Kate Hardy
A PREGNANT NURSE'S CHRISTMAS WISH	Meredith Webber

 MILLS & BOON®

Pure reading pleasure

0308 LP 2P P1 Medical

MEDICAL™

Large Print

July

THE ITALIAN'S NEW-YEAR MARRIAGE WISH	Sarah Morgan
THE DOCTOR'S LONGED-FOR FAMILY	Joanna Neil
THEIR SPECIAL-CARE BABY	Fiona McArthur
THEIR MIRACLE CHILD	Gill Sanderson
SINGLE DAD, NURSE BRIDE	Lynne Marshall
A FAMILY FOR THE CHILDREN'S DOCTOR	Dianne Drake

August

THE DOCTOR'S BRIDE BY SUNRISE	Josie Metcalfe
FOUND: A FATHER FOR HER CHILD	Amy Andrews
A SINGLE DAD AT HEATHERMERE	Abigail Gordon
HER VERY SPECIAL BABY	Lucy Clark
THE HEART SURGEON'S SECRET SON	Janice Lynn
THE SHEIKH SURGEON'S PROPOSAL	Olivia Gates

September

THE SURGEON'S FATHERHOOD SURPRISE	Jennifer Taylor
THE ITALIAN SURGEON CLAIMS HIS BRIDE	Alison Roberts
DESERT DOCTOR, SECRET SHEIKH	Meredith Webber
A WEDDING IN WARRAGURRA	Fiona Lowe
THE FIREFIGHTER AND THE SINGLE MUM	Laura Iding
THE NURSE'S LITTLE MIRACLE	Molly Evans

MILLS & BOON®

Pure reading pleasure

0308 LP 2P P2 Medical